The Rover Boys on the River
By
Arthur Winfield

INTRODUCTION

My dear boys: "The Rover Boys on the River" is a complete story in itself, but forms the ninth volume of "The Rover Boys Series for Young Americans."

Nine volumes! What a great number of tales to write about one set of characters! When I started the series I had in mind, as I have mentioned before, to write three, or possibly, four books. But the gratifying reception given to "The Rover Boys at School," soon made the publishers call for the second, third, and fourth volumes, and then came the others, and still the boys and girls do not seem to be satisfied. I am told there is a constant cry for "more! more!" and so I present this new Rover Boys story, which tells of the doings of Dick, Tom, and Sam and their friends during an outing on one of our great rivers,—an outing full of excitement and fun and with a touch of a rather unusual mystery. During the course of the tale some of the old enemies of the Rover Boys turn up, but our heroes know, as of old, how to take care of themselves; and all ends well.

In placing this book into the hands of my young readers I wish once more to thank them for the cordial reception given the previous volumes. Many have written to me personally about them, and I have perused the letters with much satisfaction. I sincerely trust the present volume fulfills their every expectation.

Affectionately and sincerely yours,

ARTHUR M. WINFIELD.

THE ROVER BOYS ON THE RIVER

CHAPTER I

PLANS FOR AN OUTING

"Whoop! hurrah! Zip, boom, ah! Rockets!"

"For gracious' sake, Tom, what's all the racket about? I thought we had all the noise we wanted last night, when we broke up camp."

"It's news, Dick, glorious news," returned Tom Rover, and he began to dance a jig on the tent flooring. "It's the best ever."

"It won't be glorious news if you bring this tent down on our heads," answered Dick Rover. "Have you discovered a gold mine?"

"Better than that, Dick. I've discovered what we are going to do with ourselves this summer."

"I thought we were going back to the farm, to rest up, now that the term at Putnam Hall is at an end."

"Pooh! Who wants to rest? I've rested all I wish right in this encampment."

"Well, what's the plan? Don't keep us in 'suspenders,' as Hans Mueller would say."

"Dear old Hansy! That Dutch boy is my heart's own!" cried Tom, enthusiastically. "I could not live without him. He must go along."

"Go along where?"

"On our outing this summer?"

"But where do you propose to go to, Tom?"

"For a trip on the broad and glorious Ohio River."

"Eh?"

"That's it, Dick. We are to sail the briny deep of that river in a houseboat. Now, what do you think of that?"

"I'd like to know what put that into your head, Tom," came from the tent opening, and Sam Rover, the youngest of the three brothers, stepped into view.

"Uncle Randolph put it into my head, not over half an hour ago, Sam. It's this way: You've heard of John V. Black of Jackville?"

"The man that owed Uncle Randolph some money?"

"Exactly. Well, Black is a bankrupt, or next door to it. He couldn't pay Uncle Randolph what was coming to him, so he turned over a houseboat instead. She's a beauty, so I am told, and she is called the *Dora*—"

"After Dora Stanhope, of course," interrupted the youngest Rover, with a quizzical look at his big brother Dick.

"Now look here, don't you start in like that, Sam," came quickly from Dick, with a blush, for the girl mentioned was his dearest friend and had been for some years. "Tell us about this houseboat, Tom," he went on.

"The houseboat is now located on the Ohio River, at a place not many miles from Pittsburg. Uncle Randolph says if we wish to we can use her this summer, and float down to the Mississippi and further yet for that matter. And we can take along half a dozen of our friends, too."

"Hurrah! that's splendid!" burst out Sam. "What a glorious way to spend the best part of this summer! Let us go, and each take a chum along."

"Father says if we go we can take Alexander Pop along to do the cooking and dirty work. The houseboat is now in charge of an old river-man named Captain Starr, who knows the Ohio and Mississippi from end to end, and we can keep him on board."

"It certainly looks inviting," mused Dick Rover. "It would take us through a section of the country we haven't as yet seen, and we might have lots of sport, fishing, and swimming, and maybe hunting. How many will the houseboat accommodate?" he added.

"Twelve or fourteen, on a pinch."

"Then we could have a jolly crowd. The question is, who are you going to take along? We can't take all of our friends, and it would seem a shame to ask some and not others."

"We can decide that question later, Dick. Remember, some of the fellows already have their arrangements made for this summer."

"I know Major Colby can't go," said Sam. "He is going to visit some relatives in Maine."

"And George Granbury is going up to the Thousand Islands with his folks," put in Tom.

"We might ask Songbird Powell," came from Dick. "I don't believe he is going anywhere in particular."

"Yes, we ought to have him by all means, and Hans Mueller, too. They would be the life of the party."

"I should like to have Fred Garrison along," said Sam. "He is always good company. We can—"

Sam broke off short as the roll of a drum was heard on the parade ground outside the tent.

"Dress parade, for the last time!" cried Dick Rover. "Come, get out and be quick about it!" And as captain of Company A he caught up his sword and buckled it on in a hurry, while Tom, as a lieutenant of the same command, did likewise.

When they came out on the parade ground of the encampment they found the cadets of Putnam Hall hurrying to the spot from all directions. It was a perfect day, this fifth of July, with the sun shining brightly and a gentle breeze blowing. The camp was as clean as a whistle, and from the tall flagstaff in front of the grounds Old Glory flapped bravely out on the air.

To those who have read "The Rover Boys at School," and other volumes in this series, Dick, Tom, and Sam need no special introduction. When at home they lived with their father and their aunt and uncle at Valley Brook farm, pleasantly located in the heart of New York State. From this farm they had been sent by their uncle Randolph to Putnam Hall military academy, presided over by Captain Victor Putnam, to whom they became warmly attached. At the academy they made many firm friends, some of whom will be introduced in the pages which follow, and also several enemies, among them Dan Baxter, the offspring of a criminal named Arnold Baxter, who, after suffering for his crimes by various terms of imprisonment, was now very sick and inclined to turn over a new leaf and become a better man.

A term at school had been followed by a remarkable chase on the ocean, and then a journey to the jungles of Africa, in a hunt after Anderson Rover, the boys' father, who

2

was missing. Then had come a trip to a gold mine in the West, followed by some exciting adventures on the Great Lakes. On an island in one of the lakes they unearthed a document relating to a treasure hidden in the Adirondack Mountains, and next made their way to that locality, in midwinter, and obtained a box containing gold, silver, and precious stones, much to their satisfaction.

After their outing in the mountains, the boys had expected to return to Putnam Hall, but a scarlet-fever scare broke out and the institution was promptly closed. This being the case, Mr. Rover thought it best to allow his sons to visit California for their health. This they did, and in the seventh volume of the series, entitled "The Rover Boys on Land and Sea," I related how Sam, Tom, and Dick were carried off to sea during a violent storm, in company with Dora Stanhope, already mentioned, and her two cousins, Nellie and Grace Laning, two particular friends of Tom and Sam. The whole party was cast away on a deserted island, and had much trouble with Dan Baxter, who joined some sailor mutineers. Our friends were finally rescued by a United States warship which chanced to pass that way and see their signal of distress.

After reaching San Francisco once more, the Rover boys had returned to the East, while Dora Stanhope and the Lanings had gone to Santa Barbara, where Mrs. Stanhope was stopping for her health. The scare at Putnam Hall was now over, and in another volume of the series, called "The Rover Boys in Camp," I related how Dick, Tom, and Sam returned to the military academy again, and took part in the annual encampment. Here there had been no end of good times and not a little hazing, the most of which was taken in good part. The boys had made a new enemy in the shape of a bully named Lew Flapp, who was finally expelled from the school for his wrong-doings. Dan Baxter also turned up, but when the authorities got after him he disappeared as quickly as he had done many times before, leaving his father to his fate, as already mentioned.

"I don't think we'll be bothered much with Dan Baxter after this," Tom had said, but he was mistaken, as later events proved.

Rat, tat, tat! Rat, tat, tat! went the drum on the parade ground, and soon the three companies which comprised the Putnam Hall Battalion were duly assembled, with Major Larry Colby in command of the whole, and Dick at the head of Company A, Fred Garrison at the head of Company B, and Mark Romer leading Company C. In front of all stood Captain Putnam, the sole owner of the military institution, and George Strong, his chief assistant.

"The boys certainly make a fine showing, on this last day of our encampment," said Captain Putnam to his assistant. "And a good deal of the credit is due to you, Mr. Strong."

"Thank you for saying so, sir," was the answer. "Yes, they look well, and I am proud of them, Captain Putnam. I believe our military school will compare favorably with any in the land."

After the drill was over Captain Putnam came forward and made a rather extended speech, in which he reviewed the work accomplished at the academy from its first opening, as told by me in another series of books, entitled "The Putnam Hall Series," starting with "The Putnam Hall Cadets," down to those later days when the Rover boys appeared on the scene. He also complimented the cadets on their excellent showing and trusted they would all have a pleasant vacation during the summer. This speech was followed by a short address by George Strong, and then came a surprise when Dick Rover stepped forward.

"Captain Putnam," said he, "in behalf of all the cadets here assembled I wish to thank you for your kind words, which we deeply appreciate.

"I have been chosen by my fellows to present you with this as a token of our esteem. We trust it will prove to your liking, and that whenever you look upon it you will remember us all."

As Dick spoke he brought into view a fair-sized package wrapped in tissue paper. When unrolled, it proved to be a small figure of a cadet, done in silver and gold. On the base was the inscription: "From the Cadets of Putnam Hall, to Their Beloved Head Master, Captain Victor Putnam."

After that Mr. Strong was presented with a set of Cooper's works and the other teachers were likewise remembered. More addresses of thanks followed, and then the battalion was dismissed for dinner.

"It's a fine wind-up for this season's encampment," said Tom, after it was over. "I don't believe we'll ever have another encampment like it."

"And now, ho, for the rolling river!" cried Sam. "Say, I'm just crazy to begin that trip on the houseboat."

"So am I," came from both of his brothers. But they might not have been so anxious had they dreamed of the many adventures and perils in store for them.

CHAPTER II
ON THE WAY TO PUTNAM HALL

"Boys, we start the march back to Putnam Hall in fifteen minutes!"

Such was the news which flew around the camp not long after the dinner hour had passed. Already the tents had been taken down, the baggage strapped, and six big wagons fairly groaned with the loads of goods to be taken back to the military institution.

The cadets had marched to the camp by one route and were to return to the academy by another. All was bustle and excitement, for in spite of the general order a few things had gone astray.

"Weally, this is most—ah—remarkable, don't you know," came from that aristocratic cadet named William Philander Tubbs.

"What's remarkable, Tublets?" asked Tom, who was near by, putting away a pair of blankets.

"Lieutenant Rover, how many times must I—ah—tell you not to address me as Tublets?" sighed the fashionable young cadet.

"Oh, all right, Tubhouse, it shan't occur again, upon my honor."

"Tubhouse! Oh, Rover, please let up!"

"What's wrong, Billy?"

"That is better, but it is bad enough," sighed William Philander. "I've—ah—lost one of my walking shoes."

"Perhaps, being a walking shoe, it walked off."

"Maybe it got in that beefsteak we had this morning," put in Sam, with a wink. "I thought that steak was rather tough."

"Shoo yourself with such a joke, Sam," came from Fred Garrison.

"Have you really lost your shoe, Tubby, dear?" sang out Songbird Powell, the so-styled "poet" of the academy. And then he started to sing:

"Rub a dub dub!
One shoe on the Tubb!
  Where can the other one be?
Look in your bunk
And look in your trunk,
  And look in the bumble-bee tree!"

"Whoop! hurrah! Songbird has composed another ode in Washtub's honor," sang out Fred Garrison. "Washtub, you ought to give Songbird a dollar for that."

"Thanks, but I make not my odes for filthy lucre," same from Powell, tragically, and then he continued:

"One penny reward,
And a big tin sword,
  To whoever finds the shoe.
Come one at a time,
And form in line,
  And raise a hullabaloo!"

And then a shout went up that could be heard all over the encampment.

"I'll lend you a slipper, Tubbs," said little Harry Moss, whose shoes were several sizes smaller than those of the aristocratic cadet.

"Somebody get me a shingle and I'll cut Tubstand a sandal with my jackknife," came from Tom.

"I'll shingle you!" roared William Philander Tubbs, and rushed away to escape his tormentors. In the end he found another shoe, but it was not the one he wanted, for that had been rolled up in the blankets by Tom and was not returned until Putnam Hall was reached.

Drums and fifes enlivened the way as the cadets started for the military academy. The march was to take the balance of that afternoon and all of the next day. During the night they were to camp out like regular soldiers on the march, in a big field Captain Putnam had hired for that purpose.

The march did not take the cadets through Oakville, so the Rover boys did not see the friends they had made in that vicinity. They headed directly for the village of Bramley, and then for another small settlement named White Corners,—why, nobody could tell, since there was not so much as a white post anywhere to be seen in that vicinity.

"It's queer how a name sticks," declared Tom, after speaking of this to his brother Dick. "They might rather call this Brown Corners, since most of the houses are brown."

At the Corners they obtained supper, which was supplied to the cadets by the hotel keeper, who had been notified in advance of their coming.

While they were eating a boy who worked around the stables of the hotel watched them curiously. Afterwards this boy came up to Sam and Tom.

"We had a cadet here yesterday who was awfully mad," said the boy.

"Had hydrophobia, eh?" returned Tom. "Too bad!"

"No, I don't mean that; I mean he was very angry."

"What was the trouble?"

"I don't know exactly, but I think he had been sent away from the school for something or other."

"What was his name?"

"Lew Flapp."

"Why, I thought he had gone home!" cried Sam.

"So did I," answered his brother. He turned to the hotel youth. "What was this Flapp doing here?"

"Nothing much. He asked the boss when you were expected here."

"Is he here now?"

"No, he left last night."

"Where did he go to?"

"I don't know, but I thought I would tell you about the fellow. I think he is going to try to do you cadets some harm."

"Did he mention any names?"

"He seemed to be extra bitter against three brothers named Rover."

"Humph!"

"Are the Rovers here?" went on the youth.

"I think they are, sonny. I'm one, this is another, and there is the third," and Tom pointed to Dick, who was at a distance, conversing with some other cadets.

"Oh, so you are the Rovers! How strange that I should speak to you of this!"

"Which way did this Lew Flapp go?" questioned Sam.

"Off the way you are bound."

"I'll wager he tries to make trouble for us on our way to Putnam Hall, Tom."

"It's not unlikely, Sam."

"Shall we tell Captain Putnam of this?" Tom shook his head.

"No, let us tell Dick, though, and a few of the others. Then we can keep our eyes peeled for Lew Flapp and, if he actually does wrong, expose him."

A little later Tom and Sam interviewed Dick on the subject, and then they told Larry Colby, Fred Garrison, George Granbury, and half a dozen others.

"I don't believe he will do much," said Larry Colby. "He is only talking, that's all. He knows well enough that Captain Putnam can have him locked up, if he wants to."

By eight o'clock that evening the field in which they were to encamp for the night was reached. Tents were speedily put up, and half a dozen camp-fires started, making the boys feel quite at home. The cadets gathered around the fires and sang song after song, and not a few practical jokes were played.

"Hans, they tell me you feel cold and want your blood shook up," said Tom to Hans Mueller, the German cadet.

"Coldt, is it?" queried Hans. "Vot you dinks, I vos coldt mid der borometer apout two hundred by der shade, ain't it? I vos so hot like I lif in Africa alretty!"

"Oh, Hans must be cold!" cried Sam. "Let us shake him up, boys!"

"All right!" came from half a dozen. "Get a blanket, somebody!"

"No, you ton't, not by my life alretty!" sang out Hans, who had been tossed up before. "I stay py der groundt mine feets on!" And he started to run away.

Several went after him, and he was caught in the middle of an adjoining cornfield, where a rough-and-tumble scuffle ensued, with poor Hans at the bottom of the heap.

"Hi, git off, kvick!" he gasped. "Dis ton't been no footsball game nohow! Git off, somebody, und dake dot knee mine mouth out of!"

"Are you warm, now, Hansy!" asked Tom.

"Chust you wait, Tom Rofer," answered the German cadet, and shook his fist at his tormentor. "I git square somedimes, or mine name ain't—"

"Sauerkraut!" finished another cadet, and a roar went up. "Hans, is it true that you eat sauerkraut three times a day when you are at home?"

"No, I ton't eat him more as dree dimes a veek," answered Hans, innocently.

"Hans is going to treat us all to Limberger cheese when his birthday comes," put in Fred Garrison. "It's a secret though, so don't tell anybody."

"I ton't vos eat Limberger," came from Hans.

"Oh, Hansy!" groaned several in chorus.

"Base villain, thou hast deceived us!" quoted Songbird Powell. "Away to the dungeon with him!" And then the crowd dragged poor Hans through the cornfield and back to the camp-fire once more, where he was made to sit so close to the blaze that the perspiration poured from his round and rosy face. Yet with it all he took the joking in good part, and often gave his tormentors as good as they sent.

"They tell me that William Philander Tubbs is going to Newport for the summer," said Tom. a little later, when the cadets were getting ready to retire. "Just wait till he gets back next Fall, he'll be more dudish than ever."

"We ought to tame him a little before we let him go," said Sam.

"Right you are, Sam. But what can we do? Nearly everything has been tried since we went into camp."

"I have a plan, Tom."

"All right; let's have it."

"Why not black Tubby up while he is asleep?"

"Sam, you are a jewel. But where are we to get the lamp-black?"

"I've got it already. I put several corks in the camp-fire, and burnt cork is the best stuff for blacking up known."

"Right again. Oh, but we'll make William Philander look like a regular negro minstrel. And that's not all. After the job is done we'll wake him up and tell him Captain Putnam wants to see him at once."

Several boys were let into the secret, and then all waited impatiently for Tubbs to retire. This he soon did, and in a few minutes was sound asleep.

6

"Now then, come on," said Sam, and led the way to carry out the anticipated fun.

CHAPTER III

THE DOINGS OF A NIGHT

As luck would have it, William Philander Tubbs just then occupied a tent alone, his two tent-mates being on guard duty for two hours as was the custom during encampment.

The aristocratic cadet lay flat on his back, with his face and throat well exposed.

"Now, be careful, Sam, or you'll wake him up," whispered Tom.

One cadet held a candle, while Sam and Tom blackened the face of the sleeping victim of the joke. The burnt cork was in excellent condition and soon William Philander looked for all the world like a coal-black darkey.

"Py chimanatics, he could go on der stage py a nigger minstrel company," was Hans Mueller's comment.

"Makes almost a better nigger than he does a white man," said Tom, dryly.

"Wait a minute till I fix up his coat for him," said Fred Garrison, and turned the garment inside out.

A moment later all of the cadets withdrew, leaving the tent in total darkness. Then one stuck his head in through the flap.

"Hi, there, Private Tubbs!" he called out. "Wake up!"

"What—ah—what's the mattah?" drawled the aristocratic cadet, sleepily.

"Captain Putnam wants you to report to him or to Mr. Strong at once," went on the cadet outside, in a heavy, assumed voice.

"Wants me to report?" questioned Tubbs, sitting up in astonishment.

"Yes, and at once. Hurry up, for it's very important."

"Well, this is assuredly strange," murmured William Philander to himself. "Wonder what is up?"

He felt around in the dark for a light, but it had been removed by Tom and so had all the matches.

"Beastly luck, not a match!" growled Tubbs, and then began to dress in the dark. In his hurry he did not notice that his coat was inside out, nor did he discover that his face and hands were blacked.

Captain Putnam's quarters were at the opposite end of the camp, and in that direction William Philander hurried until suddenly stopped by a guard who chanced to be coming in from duty.

"Halt!" cried the cadet. "What are you doing in this camp?" he demanded.

"Captain Putnam wants me," answered Tubbs, thinking the guard wanted to know why he was astir at that hour of the night.

"Captain Putnam wants you?"

"Yes."

"It's strange. How did you get in?"

"In? In where?"

"In this camp?"

"Oh, Ribble, are you crazy?"

"So you know me," said Ribble. "Well, I must say I don't know you."

"You certainly must be crazy. I am William Philander Tubbs."

"What! Oh, then you—" stammered Ribble, and then a light dawned on him. "Who told you the captain wanted to see you?"

"Some cadet who just woke me up."

"All right, go ahead then," and Ribble grinned. Behind Tubbs he now saw half a dozen cadets hovering in the semi-darkness, watching for sport.

On ran William Philander, to make up for lost time, and soon arrived at the flap of the tent occupied by Captain Putnam.

"Here I am, Captain Putnam!" he called out. And then, as he got no reply, he called again. By this time the captain was awake, and coming to the flap, he peered out.

7

"What do you want?" he asked, sharply.

"You sent for me, sir," stammered Tubbs.

"I sent for you?"

"Yes, sir."

"I have no recollection of so doing," answered Captain Putman. "Where are you from?"

"From?"

"Exactly."

"Why, I am—ah—from this camp," answered the puzzled Tubbs.

"Do you mean to tell me you belong here?" questioned the now astonished master of Putnam Hall.

"Of course, Captain Putnam. Didn't you send for me? Somebody said you did," continued William Philander.

"Sir, I don't know you and never heard of you, so far as I can remember. You must be mixed up.

"I mixed up? I guess you are mixed up," roared Tubbs, growing angry.

"If I don't belong to this camp, where do I belong?"

"How should I know? We have no negroes here, to the best of my knowledge."

"Captain Putnam, what do you mean by calling me an—ah—negro?" fumed William Philander.

"Well, aren't you one? I can't see very well."

"No, sir; I am not a negro, and never was a negro," answered Tubbs, getting more and more excited. "I shall report this to my parents when I arrive home."

"Will you in all goodness tell me your name?" queried Captain Putnam, beginning to realize that something was wrong.

"You know my name well enough, sir."

"Perhaps I do, and perhaps I don't. Answer me, please."

"My name is William Philander Tubbs."

"Tubbs! Is it possible!"

"Somebody came to my tent and said you wanted to see me."

"Well, did you think it was necessary to black up to make a call on me?"

"Black up?" repeated William Philander. "That is what I said?"

"Am I black, sir?"

"Yes, as black as coal. Look at yourself in this glass," and the captain held out a small looking glass and also a lantern.

When Tubbs saw himself in the glass he almost had a fit.

"My gracious sakes alive!" he groaned. "How ridiculous! How did this happen? Why, I look like a negro!"

"Is anything amiss, Captain Putnam?" came from the next tent, and George Strong appeared.

"Nothing, excepting that Private Tubbs has seen fit to black up as a negro and call upon me," answered the master of the academy, with a faint smile playing around the corners of his mouth.

"I didn't black up!" roared William Philander. "It's all a horrid joke somebody has played on me while I was asleep! You don't want me, do you?"

"No, Tubbs."

"Then I'll go back, and if I can find out who did this—"

A burst of laughter from a distance made him break off short.

"They're laughing at me!" he went on. "Just hear that!"

"Go to bed, and I will investigate in the morning," answered Captain Putnam, and William Philander went off, vowing vengeance.

"Just wait till I find out who did it," he told himself, as he washed up the best he could in some cold water. "I'll have them in court for it." But he never did find out, nor did Captain Putnam's investigation lead to any disclosures.

William Philander's trials for that night were not yet at an end. On the march to the camp some of the cadets had picked up a number of burrs of fair size. A liberal quantity of these had been introduced under the covers of Tubbs' cot immediately after he left the tent.

Having washed up as best he could, the aristocratic cadet blew out the light he had borrowed and prepared to retire once more. He threw back the covers and dropped heavily upon the cot in just the spot where the sharpest of the burrs lay.

An instant later a wild shriek of pain and astonishment rent the air.

"Ouch! Oh my, I'm stuck full of pins! Oh, dear me!"

And then William Philander Tubbs leaped up and began to dance around like a wild Indian.

"What's the matter with you, Billy?" asked one of his tent-mates, entering in the midst of the excitement.

"What's the matter?" roared poor Tubbs. "Everything is the matter, don't you know. It's an ah—outrage!"

"Somebody told me you had blacked up as a negro minstrel and were going to serenade your best girl."

"It's not so, Parkham. Some beastly cadets played a joke on me! Oh, wait till I find out who did it!" And then William Philander began to moan once more over the burrs. It was a good quarter of an hour before he had his cot cleaned off and fit to use once more, and even then he was so excited and nervous he could not sleep another wink.

"William Philander won't forget his last night with the boys in a hurry," remarked Tom, as he slipped off to bed once more.

"You had better keep quiet over this," came from Dick. "We don't want to spoil our records for the term, remember."

"Right you are, Dick. I'll be as mum as a clam climbing a huckleberry bush."

The boys were tired out over the march of the afternoon and over playing the joke on Tubbs, and it was not long before all of the Rovers were sound asleep. The three brothers had begged for permission to tent together and this had been allowed by Captain Putnam, for the term was virtually over, ending with the dismissal of the cadets at the last encampment parade.

On guard duty at one end of the field was a cadet named Link Smith, a rather weak-minded fellow who was easily led by those who cared to exert an influence over him. At one time Link Smith had trained with Lew Flapp and his evil associates, but fortunately for the feeble-minded cadet he had been called home during the time when Lew Flapp got into the trouble which ended by his dismissal from Putnam Hall.

Link Smith was pacing up and down sleepily when he heard a peculiar whistle close at hand. He listened intently and soon heard the whistle repeated.

"The old call," he murmured to himself. At first he did not feel like answering, but presently did so. Then from out of the gloom stalked a tall young fellow, dressed in the uniform of a cadet but with a face that was strangely painted and powdered.

"Who is it?" questioned Link Smith, uneasily.

"Don't you know me, Link?"

"Lew Flapp!" cried the weak-minded cadet.

"Hush, not so loud, Link. Somebody might hear you."

"What do you want?"

"I want to visit the camp," answered Lew Flapp.

CHAPTER IV
WHAT THE MORNING BROUGHT FORTH

Link Smith was much surprised by Lew Flapp's assertion that he wanted to visit the camp during the middle of the night and when practically everybody was asleep.

"What do you want to come in for?" he asked, feeling fairly certain that Flapp's mission could not be as upright and honest as desired.

"Oh, it's all right, Link," answered the big bully, smoothly.

"But what do you want?"

"Well, if you must know, I want to talk to a couple of my old friends."

"Why can't you talk to them to-morrow, after they leave school?"

"That won't do. I want them to do something for me before they leave the academy."

"It's a strange request to make, Lew."

"Oh, it's perfectly square, I assure you. You see, it's this way: I want them to get some proofs for me,—to prove that I am not as black as the follows reported to Captain Putnam."

Now, it is possible that some other cadet would not have been hoodwinked in this fashion by the bully, but Link Smith swallowed the explanation without a second thought.

"Oh, if that's what you want, go ahead," said he. "But don't tell anybody I let you in."

"I shan't say a word if you don't," answered Lew Flapp. "By the way," he went on, with assumed indifference, "they tell me the Rover boys have cleared out and gone home."

"No, they haven't," was Link Smith's prompt answer.—They are right here."

"Are you sure, Link?"

"Of course I am. They are bunking together in the last tent in Street B, over yonder," and the feeble-minded cadet pointed with his hand as he spoke.

"Is that so! Well, I don't care. I don't want to see them again until I can prove to Captain Putnam that they are a set of rascals."

"Are you going to try to get into the academy again, Lew?" asked Link, curiously.

"Not much! I'll be done with Captain Putnam just as soon as I can show him how he mistreated me and how the Rovers are pulling the wool over his eyes."

"Everybody here thinks the Rovers about perfect."

"That's because they don't know them as well as I and Rockley do."

A few words more passed, and then Lew Flapp slipped into the camp lines and made his way between the long rows of tents.

He had gained from Link Smith just the information he desired, namely, the location of the Rover boys' sleeping quarters. He looked back, to make certain that Link was not watching him, and then hurried on to where the Rovers rested, totally unconscious of the proximity of their enemy.

"I'll show them what I can do," muttered Lew Flapp to himself. "I'll make them wish they had never been born!"

At last the tent was reached and with caution he opened the flap and peered inside. All was dark, and with a hand that was none too steady he struck a match and held it up.

Each of the Rover boys lay sleeping peacefully on his cot, with his clothing hung up on one of the tent poles.

"Now for working my little plan," murmured Flapp, and allowed the match to go out. In a second more he was inside the tent, moving around cautiously so as not to disturb the sleepers.

The bully remained in the tent all of ten minutes. Then he came out as cautiously as he had entered, and fairly ran to where Link Smith was still on guard.

"Did you see them?" asked the feeble-minded cadet.

"I did, and it's all right, Link. Now, don't tell anybody I visited the camp."

"Humph! do you think I want to get myself in trouble?"

"Good-night."

"Good-night."

And in a moment more Lew Flapp was out of sight down the country roadway and Link Smith was pacing his post as before.

Bright and early the camp was astir, and at half-past seven o'clock a good hot breakfast was served, the cadets pitching into the food provided with a will.

10

"And now for Putnam Hall and the grand wind-up," said Tom, as he finished his repast.

"And then to go home and prepare for that grand trip on the houseboat," came from Sam.

"Which puts me in mind that we must see who will go with us," said Dick.

"Songbird Powell says he is more than willing," answered Tom. "And I know Dutchy will fall all over himself to become one of the party."

"I think Fred Garrison will go," said Sam. "He said he would let me know as soon as he heard from his parents."

Captain Putnam had expected to begin the march to the Hall by half-past eight, but there were numerous delays in packing the camping outfit, so the battalion was not ready for the start until over an hour later.

The cadets were just being formed to start the march when several men appeared at the edge of the field.

"There's them young soldiers now!" cried one. Come on and find the rascals!"

"What do you want, gentlemen?" demanded George Strong, who happened to be near the crowd.

"Who is in charge of this school?" asked one of the men.

"Captain Victor Putnam is the owner. I am his head assistant."

"Well, I'm Josiah Cotton, the constable of White Corners."

"What can I do for you, Mr. Cotton?"

"I'm after a feller named Dick Rover, and his two brothers. Are they here?"

"They are. What do you want of them?"

"I'm goin' to lock 'em up if they did what I think they did."

"Lock them up?" cried George Strong, in astonishment.

"That's what I said. Show me the young villains."

"But what do you think they have done?"

"They broke into my shop an' stole some things," put in another of the men.

"That's right, they did," came from a third man. "Don't let 'em give ye the slip, Josiah."

"I ain't a-goin' to let 'em give me the slip," growled the constable from White Corners.

"When was your shop robbed?" demanded George Strong, of the man who had said he was the sufferer.

"I can't say exactly, fer I was to the city, a-buying of more goods."

"Mr. Fairchild is a jeweler and watchmaker, besides dealing in paints, oils, glass, an' wall paper," explained the constable. "He carries a putty considerable stock of goods as are valuable. Yesterday, or early last night, when he was away, his shop was broken into and robbed."

"And what makes you think the Rovers are the thieves?" asked George Strong.

"We got proof," came doggedly from Aaron Fairchild. "We're certain on it."

By this time, seeing that something was wrong, Captain Putnam came to the scene. In the meantime the battalion was already formed, with Major Colby at the head and Dick in his proper position as captain of Company A.

"I cannot, believe that the Rover Boys are guilty of this robbery," said the master of Putnam Hall after listening to what the newcomers had to say. "What proof have you that they did it?"

"This proof, for one thing," answered Josiah Cotton, and drew from his pocket a memorandum book and the envelope to a letter. In the front of the memorandum book was the name, Richard Rover, and the envelope was addressed likewise.

"The thief dropped that," went on the constable.

11

"Where did you find these things?"

"On the floor of the shop, in front of the desk."

"Anybody might have dropped them."

"See here, Captain Putnam, do you stand up fer shieldin' a thief?" roared Aaron Fairchild. "To me this hull thing is as plain as the nose on my face."

As Aaron Fairchild's smelling organ was an unusually large one, this caused the master of Putnam Hall to smile. But he immediately grew grave again.

"This is a serious matter, Mr. Fairchild. I do not wish to shield a thief, but at the same time I cannot see one or more of my pupils unjustly treated."

"Are ye afraid to have 'em examined?"

"By no means. I will call them up and you can talk to them. But I advise you to be careful of what you say. The Rover boys come from a family that is rich, and they can make it exceedingly warm for you if you accuse them wrongfully."

"Oh, I know what I'm a-doin' and the constable knows what he's a-doin', too," answered Aaron Fairchild.

George Strong was sent to summon Dick, Tom, and Sam, and soon came up with the three brothers behind him.

"Something is wrong, that is certain," murmured Dick.

"Those men look mad enough to chew us up," answered Tom.

"Now, boys, keep cool," cautioned George Strong. "I think some terrible mistake has been made."

"What's it all about, Mr. Strong?" asked Sam.

"I'll let them explain," returned the head assistant.

Josiah Cotton had heard Captain Putnam's words of caution to Aaron Fairchild, and as he had a great regard for persons who were rich, and did not want to get himself into trouble, he resolved to move with caution.

"I'd like to ask you three young gents a few questions," said he, as the boys came up. "Fust, which one of you is Richard Rover?"

"I am Richard, commonly called Dick," was the ready reply. "This is my brother Tom, and this is Sam."

"Very well. Now then, do you remember visitin' Mr. Fairchild's jewelry an' paint store?" went on the constable.

"Visiting a jewelry and paint store?" repeated Dick. "I do not. What a combination!"

"Perhaps he paints his jewels," put in the fun-loving Tom.

"Don't you git funny with us!" growled Aaron Fairchild. "Let's come to the p'int. My store was robbed, an' I'm thinking you fellers done the deed."

"Robbed!" echoed Sam.

"And you think we did it," put in Dick, indignantly. "I like that!"

"We are not thieves," said Tom. "And you ought to have your head punched for thinking it."

"Boys, keep cool," came from Captain Putnam. "Mr. Cotton, hadn't you better do the talking for Mr. Fairchild?"

"I want 'em searched," burst out Aaron Fairchild. "If they robbed my store they must have put the stuff somewheres."

"What makes you think we robbed you?" asked Dick.

"This," and he was shown the memorandum book and the envelope.

"Humph! I lost that book some weeks ago, when I had my fight with Lew Flapp, Rockley, and the rest of that crowd that were dismissed from the academy."

"And what of the envelope, Richard?" asked Captain Putnam.

"I don't remember anything about that. It probably came on a letter from home and I must have thrown it away."

"The book and the envelope were found on the floor of the shop that was robbed."

"Well, I didn't drop them there."

12

"And neither did I," came from Tom.

"Nor I," added Sam.

"Are you going to let us search you and your belongings or not?" demanded the constable from White Corners.

"I don't see why you should search us," put in Tom, hotly. "It's an outrage, to my way of thinking."

"You had better let him make a search," came from Captain Putnam. "Then he will see that he has made a mistake."

"All right, search me all you please," said Sam.

"I am of Tom's opinion, that it is an outrage," said Dick. "Nevertheless, he can search me if he wishes."

"Let us retire to yonder barn, out of the sight of the battalion," said Captain Putnam.

The constable and Aaron Fairchild were willing, and all walked to the barn in question.

"You can look at that first," said Dick, and unbuttoning his coat he took it off and handed it to the constable.

Josiah Cotton dove into one pocket after another, bringing out various articles which were Dick's private property.

"Any o' these yours?" he asked the jeweler.

"Can't say as they are, Josiah," answered Aaron Fairchild. "Go on a-huntin'. Maybe somethin' is in the linin'."

"There is!" shouted the constable, running his hand over the padding. He found a small hole and put in his fingers. "Here ye are!" he ejaculated, and brought forth two plain gold rings and one set with a topaz.

"My property!" gasped Aaron Fairchild. "My property and I'll swear to it! Didn't I tell ye he was a thief?"

CHAPTER V
FOR AND AGAINST

All in the barn gazed in amazement at the three rings which the constable of White Corners held in his hand.

"I don't know how those rings got into my coat," said Dick, who was the first to recover from the shock.

"I am certain Dick didn't steal them," put in Tom.

"And so am I," added Sam. "Dick, this is a plot against you."

"It ain't no plot—it's plain facts," came from Aaron Fairchild. "Go on an' continue the search, Josiah."

"That's what I'm a-doin'," returned the constable.

He felt the coat over carefully and presently brought forth another ring and a pair of child's bracelets.

"It's as plain as preachin'!" came from the third man, a farmer named Gassam. "He's the thief, sure."

"I declare upon my honor I am innocent," cried Dick, the hot blood rushing to his face. He turned to Captain Putnam. "You don't think I—I—"

"I believe what you say, Captain Rover," answered the master of the Hall, promptly. "There is assuredly some mistake here."

"Give me your coat," said Josiah Cotton to Tom.

The garment was handed over, and after a thorough search two small gold stick pins were found in the middle of the back.

"More o' my goods," cried Aaron Fairchild, triumphantly. "I can prove I had 'em on sale not four days ago."

Sam's coat was then examined, and from one of the sleeves came half a dozen cheap rings and an equally cheap watchchain.

"All mine. The case is as clear as day," said the jeweler. "Josiah, you must lock 'em up."

"0' course I'll lock 'em up," answered the constable.

"Lock us up!" cried Sam, aghast.

"Not much!" came from Tom. "I'm no thief, and I don't propose to go to jail."

"Boys, have you any idea how this jewelry got into your clothes?" asked Captain Putnam.

"No, sir," came promptly from the three.

The rest of the Rover boys' clothing was then searched and a few more cheap rings were brought to light.

"Now let us go for their baggage," said the constable, and this was done, but nothing more was found.

It was soon buzzing around the battalion, which stood at parade rest, that something was wrong, and then somebody whispered that the Rovers were accused of breaking into a shop and stealing some jewelry.

"It can't be true," said Fred Garrison. "I shall never believe it." And a number of others said the same. But a few shrugged their shoulders— those who had belonged to the Lew Flapp and Dan Baxter crowd.

"I never trusted those Rovers altogether," said one. "They have too much money to spend."

"Well, they are worth a good bit of money," replied another cadet.

"This ain't a quarter of the stuff I lost," said Aaron Fairchild, after the baggage had undergone a rigid inspection.

"What have you done with the rest?" asked the constable of the Rovers.

"You may think as you please," said Dick. "I am innocent and I do not understand how that stuff got where you found it. An enemy must have placed it there."

"Yes, and that enemy must be the one who robbed the shop!" cried Tom.

"It's easy enough to talk," came from Gassam, the farmer. "But you can't go behind the evidence, as they say in court. You might just as well confess, an' give up the rest o' the goods. Maybe if ye do that, they'll let ye off easy."

"What do you consider this stuff worth?" asked Dick.

"Nigh on to thirty-five dollars," answered Aaron Fairchild.

"How much did you lose altogether?"

"About a hundred an' sixty dollars' worth."

"Then the real thief kept about a hundred and twenty-five dollars' worth for himself," said Tom.

"There can be no doubt but that one of our enemies did this," said Sam. "The question is, which one?"

"Perhaps Dan Baxter—or Lew Flapp," suggested Dick.

"Yes, but how did the things get into our clothes, Tom?"

"I give it up."

"That sort of talk won't wash," put in the constable. "You have got to go with me."

"Where to?"

"To Squire Haggerty's office."

"I will go with you," said Captain Putnam. "This affair must be sifted to the bottom."

It was learned that Squire Haggerty lived two miles away. But a wagon was handy, belonging to a nearby farmer, and this was hired to take the whole party to the place.

"You must take charge of the cadets," said Captain Putnam to his head assistant. "I must see this affair through."

"I do not believe the Rovers are guilty, sir," whispered George Strong.

"Neither do I. This is a plot against them. The question is, who carried the plot out?"

Not long after this the battalion of cadets marched off on the road to Putnam Hall while the Rovers and the others entered the big wagon.

Inside of half an hour Squire Haggerty's home was reached. The squire proved to be an Irishman of about fifty, who when he was not acting as a judge did jobs of mason work in the vicinity.

"Sure, an' it's the boldest robbery we have had in this neighborhood for years," said the squire. "The back door av the shop was broken open and many valuables extracted from the premises."

"Have you any idea when the robbery was committed?" asked Captain Putnam.

"Not exactly Mr. Fairchild was away all day yesterday and did not get home until nearly twelve o'clock at night."

"Didn't he leave anybody else to run the shop?"

"He has nobody. When he goes away he has to lock up."

All were ushered into the squire's parlor, where he had a flat-top desk and several office chairs. The squire had heard of Captain Putnam, and knew of the fame of the academy, and he respected the Hall owner accordingly.

"I will be after hearing all the particulars of this case," said he, as he sat down to his desk.

In a long, rambling story Aaron Fairchild told how he had come home from a visit to the city late the night before. He had some goods for his shop with him and on going to the place had found the back door broken in and everything in the shop in confusion. Jewelry and other things to the value of a hundred and sixty dollars had been taken, and on the floor he had found the memorandum book and the envelope. From some boys in the hamlet he has learned that the Rover boys belonged to the Putnam Hall cadets, and farmer Gassam had told him where to find the young soldiers. Then he had called up the constable and set out; with the results already related.

"This certainly looks black for the Rover boys," said Squire Haggerty. "How do ye account for having the goods on your persons, tell me that now?"

"I can account for it only in one way," said Dick. "The thief, whoever he was, placed them there, for the double purpose of keeping suspicion from himself and to get us into trouble."

"Thin, if he wanted to git you into throuble, he was after being a fellow who had a grudge against ye?"

"That must be it," put in Captain Putnam.

"Do ye know of any such persons?"

"Yes, there are a number of such persons," answered Dick. And he mentioned Dan Baxter, Flapp, Rockley, and a number of others who in the past had proved to be his enemies.

Following this, Captain Putnam related how Dan Baxter had escaped after trying to harm Dick Rover and how it was that Lew Flapp was considered an enemy and how the fellow had been dismissed from the academy, along with several followers. Squire Haggerty listened attentively.

"Well, if one of thim fellows robbed the shop he must have visited your camp, too," said Squire Haggerty. "Did ye see any of thim around?"

Captain Putnam looked inquiringly at the Rover boys.

"I must confess I didn't see any of them," said Dick.

"But we heard from Lew Flapp," cried Tom, suddenly. "How strange that I didn't think of this before."

"Where did you hear from him, Thomas?"

"At the hotel where we stopped for supper yesterday. A boy who works around the stables told me Flapp had been there and was very angry because he had been sent away from the academy. The boy said Flapp vowed he was going to get square with the Rovers for what they had done."

15

"What boy was that?" asked Josiah Cotton, with interest.

The boy was described and, a little later, he was brought over from the hotel. He was very much frightened and insisted upon it that he had had nothing to do with the robbery.

"Tell what you can about Lew Flapp," said Dick, and the boy did so.

"That young fellow had been drinking, or else he wouldn't have talked so much," added the lad. "He certainly said he was going to get square with the Rover brothers."

"Have you seen him since?"

"Yes, I saw him in the village right after the cadets left."

"Anywhere near Mr. Fairchild's shop?"

"On the road that runs back of the shop."

"Where was he going?"

"I don't know."

"And that is the last you saw of him?"

"Yes, sir."

"You don't know if he went towards the back of the shop?"

"No, sir."

More than this the boy could not tell and he was excused. Squire Haggerty shook his head in perplexity.

"I don't know about this," he said. "But it looks to me as if I'll have to hold these Rover brothers until they can clear themselves."

CHAPTER VI
LINK SMITH'S CONFESSION

For a moment there was a painful pause and the Rover boys looked at each other and at Captain Putnam in perplexity.

"Does this mean that we must go to jail?" demanded Tom.

"I don't think it will be necessary to hold them," came from Captain Putnam. "Squire Haggerty, I presume you know who I am."

"Yes, sir, Captain Putnam of Putnam Hall."

"Then you will, of course, let me go on a bail bond for these three pupils of mine."

"If ye care to do it, captain."

"Certainly. I am convinced that they are innocent. Why, it is preposterous to think that they would break into such a shop and rob it of a hundred and sixty dollars' worth of goods. They are rich young gentlemen, of a high-standing family, and each has all the spending money he needs."

"I see, I see."

"Well, it ain't nuthin' to me what they be, so long as I git my goods back," growled Aaron Fairchild. "I ain't got nuthin' against 'em personally, especially if they are innocent."

"I think you will find it to your advantage to let this whole matter rest for the present," went on Captain Putnam. "If you make a charge against the boys it will hurt both them and my school. I feel sure they will not run away, and I will give you my personal word that they shall appear in court whenever wanted."

"That sounds reasonable," came from the constable, who was beginning to fear the influence which Captain Putnam and the Rovers might bring to bear on the case. "It ain't no nice thing to ruin a boy's repertation, if he ain't guilty," he added.

"That is a sensible speech which does you credit, sir," said the captain.

"I'd like to find this feller Flapp," went on Aaron Fairchild. "How does he look?"

"I have his photograph at the academy. I will let the constable have that, if he wishes it."

"That suits me," returned Josiah Cotton. "Hang me if I don't kinder think he must be guilty. But it puzzles me how them things got in the boys' uniforms."

The matter was discussed for fully an hour, and the whole party visited Aaron Fairchild's shop. But no clews were brought to light. Then a wagon was hired to take the

16

captain and the boys to Putnam Hall. The constable went along, to get the photograph which had been promised.

On the way the three Rovers were unusually silent and but little was said by the master of the school. Arriving at the Hall the picture was turned over to Josiah Cotton, who soon after departed. Then the three Rovers were invited into the captain's private office. The marching battalion had not yet arrived and was not expected for several hours.

"I'd like to sift this matter out," said the captain, seating himself at his desk. "Richard, when did you clean your uniform last?"

"Yesterday afternoon, Captain Putnam."

"Were those holes in there then?"

"I don't think so."

"How about your uniform, Thomas?"

"I cleaned up yesterday morning. I don't remember any holes."

"And you, Samuel?"

"I had a hole in my left sleeve, but the jewelry was found in the right sleeve."

"Let me examine the coats."

This was done, and all concluded that the holes had been cut with the blade of a sharp knife, or with a small pair of scissors.

"I believe the job was done in the dark," said Dick. "Somebody must have visited our tent last night after we went to sleep."

"When did you go to sleep, Richard?"

"Well, I don't think we were real sound asleep until about midnight. There was some sort of a noise in the camp that kept us awake."

"Somebody said Tubbs was up playing negro minstrel," added Tom, soberly.

"Yes, he was up. So you went to sleep about midnight? And when did you get up?"

"At the first call," answered Sam.

"And your coats were as you had left them?"

"Mine was," came from Sam and Dick.

"I don't remember exactly how I did leave mine," said Tom. "But I didn't notice anything unusual."

"Then, if the real thief visited our camp he must have come in between midnight and six o'clock," went on the master of the school. "I must question those who were on guard duty about this."

"That's the idea!" cried Dick. "If the thief sneaked in somebody must have seen him."

"Unless a guard was asleep on his post," came from Tom. "As it was the last night out they may have been pretty lax in that direction."

Dinner had been ordered, and the three Rovers dined with the captain in his private dining room. Then the boys went up to their dormitory to pack their trunks.

"I must say this is a fine ending for the term," was Tom's comment, as he began to get his belongings out of the closet. "And after everything looked so bright, too!"

"It's a jolly shame!" cried Sam. "If Lew Flapp did this, or Dan Baxter, I'd like to—to wring his neck for it!"

"It will certainly put a cloud on our name," said Dick. "In spite of what we can say, some folks will be mean enough to think we are guilty."

"We must catch the thief and make him confess," went on Tom.

The three boys packed their trunks and other belongings and then went below again and down to the gymnasium and then to the boathouse. But they could not interest themselves in anything and their manner showed it.

"What is the matter that you came back so soon?" questioned Mrs. Green, the matron of the academy, who knew them well.

"Oh, we had business with Captain Putnam," answered Tom, and that was all he' would say. He dearly loved to play jokes on the matron, but now he felt too downcast to give such things a thought.

Late in the afternoon the distant rattle of drums was heard, and soon the battalion, dusty and hot, came into view, making a splendid showing as it swung up the broad roadway leading to the Hall.

"Here they come!" cried Sam. But he had not any heart to meet his friends, and kept out of sight until the young cadets came to a halt and were dismissed for the last time by Captain Putnam and Major Colby.

"Well, this is certainly strange," said Larry Colby, as he came up to Dick. "What was the row in the barn about?"

"I'll have to tell you some other time, Larry," was Dick's answer. "There has been trouble and Captain Putnam wants to get at the bottom of it."

"Somebody said you had been locked up for robbing a jewelry shop."

"There has been a robbery and we were suspected. But we were not locked up."

As soon as he was able to do so, Captain Putnam learned the names of the twelve cadets who had been on picket duty between midnight and six o'clock that morning. These cadets were marched to one of the classrooms and interviewed one at a time in the captain's private office.

From the first six cadets to go in but little was learned. One cadet, when told that something of a very serious nature had occurred—something which was not a mere school lark and could not be overlooked—confessed that he had allowed two cadets to slip out of camp and come back again with two capfuls of apples taken from a neighboring orchard.

"But I can't tell their names, Captain Putnam," the cadet added.

"How long were they gone, Beresford?"

"Not over fifteen or twenty minutes."

"Did you see the apples?"

"Yes, sir, I—er—ate two of them."

"And you allowed nobody else to pass?"

"No, sir."

"Very well; you may go," and Beresford went, thankful that he had not been reprimanded for neglect of duty. Had the thing occurred in the middle of the term the reprimand would surely have been forthcoming.

The next cadet to come in was Link Smith, who showed by his general manner that he was much worried. Captain Putnam knew Smith thoroughly and also remembered that the feeble-minded cadet was a fellow easily led astray.

"Smith, you were on guard duty from twelve o'clock to two last night," he began severely.

"Yes, sir," answered Link Smith, with an inward shiver.

"Did you fall asleep on your post during that time?"

"No, sir—that is, I don't think I did."

"What do you mean by saying you don't think you did?"

"I—that is—I was awfully sleepy and could scarcely keep my eyes open. I—I sat down on a rock for a little while."

"And slept?

"I—I think not."

"Was that before or after you allowed an outsider to get into our camp?"

"Oh, Captain Putnam, how did you know I let somebody in? I—that is—I mean, who said I let anybody in?" stammered poor Smith, taken completely off his guard.

"Never mind who told me. What I want to know is, did you sleep after you let him in or before?"

"Why, I—I—really—"

"Tell me the truth, Smith."

"I guess I took a nap afterwards, sir. But it was only for a minute, sir," pleaded the cadet.

"I see. Did you see the outsider leave camp after you had let him in?"

"Why, sir—I—I—"

"I want the strict truth, remember, Smith. If you don't tell the truth you may get yourself in great trouble."

"Oh, Captain Putnam, I—I didn't mean to do anything wrong!"

"Did you see the outsider leave again or not?"

"Yes, sir, I saw him leave?"

"How soon after he had come in?"

"About fifteen or twenty minutes,—certainly, not much longer than that."

"Now, who was the outsider?"

"Why, I—er—I—"

"Answer me, Smith!" And now Captain Putnam's voice was as keen as the blade of a knife. He stood before the frightened cadet, looking him squarely in the eyes.

"It was Lew Flapp. But, oh, please, don't let him know I told you! He'll kill me if he finds it out!" Link Smith was about ready to cry.

"Lew Flapp." The captain drew a long breath. "How did you come to let him in? You knew he had been dismissed from the school."

"He begged me to let him in, saying he merely wanted to speak to two of his old friends. I asked him why he didn't wait until morning, but he said he wanted them to do something for him before they left the school—that he must see them then and there."

"Did he mention his friends' names?"

"No, sir."

"What did he say when he went away?"

"Nothing much, sir, excepting that he had seen them and it was all right."

"Where did he go to?"

"I don't know. It was dark and I soon lost sight of him."

"He came alone?"

"Yes, sir. But, please, Captain Putnam, don't tell him I told you, or he'll kill me."

"Don't be alarmed, Smith. I'll protect you. If you see Flapp again tell me at once."

"I will, sir."

This ended the examination of Link Smith, and as soon as it was over the remainder of the cadets who had been on guard duty the night before were likewise told they might go.

CHAPTER VII
FUN ON THE CAMPUS

"It was Lew Flapp, just as I supposed," said Dick, when he heard the news from Captain Putnam. "What a rascal he is getting to be! Almost as bad as Dan Baxter."

"Oh, he would have to be a good deal worse than he is to be as bad as Dan," returned Sam. "But I admit, he is bad enough."

"I'd give some money to lay my hands on him," put in Tom. "Oh, but wouldn't I punch his head good and hand him over to the police afterwards!"

Word was sent to Josiah Cotton and other officers of the law to look for Flapp, but for the time being nothing was seen or heard of that individual.

The Rover boys were to start for home the next day and that night a large number of the cadets held a special jollification on the parade ground in front of the Hall. A bonfire was lit, and the lads danced around and sang to their hearts' content.

In the midst of the excitement somebody saw Peleg Snuggers, the general-utility man of the school, hurrying across the backyard.

"Hullo, there goes Peleg!" was the shout.

"Let's give him a rousing farewell, boys," came from Tom Rover. "Hi, there, Peleg, come here."

"Can't, I'm in a hurry," responded the man-of-all-work, who had had the cadets plague him before.

"Oh, you must come," was the cry, and in a moment more Peleg Snuggers was surrounded.

"Let us march him around on our shoulders," went on Tom. "Peleg loves that, I know he does."

"Don't, neither!" cried the general-utility man. "Now, Tom Rover, you just let me alone."

"We'll carry you around for your rheumatism, Peleg. You've got rheumatism, haven't you?"

"No, I haven't."

"It's good for the lumbago, too."

"Ain't got no lumba—Oh, crickey! Let me down, boys. I don't want a ride!"

"Behold, the conquering hero comes!" announced Sam, as six of the boys hoisted poor Snuggers up into the air. "Now, sit up straight, Peleg. Don't you want a sword?"

"Here's a broom," put in Fred Garrison, and handed over an article which was worn to a stump. "Present arms! Forward, march! General Washtub will lead the funeral procession."

"If you let me tumble I'll break my neck!" gasped Peleg Snuggers. "Oh, creation! How can I carry that broom and hold on, too! This is awful! Shall I call the captain? Let up, I say!"

"Send for Mrs. Green to give him some soothing syrup, he's got the fits," came from a cadet in the crowd.

"I'll get her," cried Tom, struck with a new idea.

Off ran the fun-loving youth to the kitchen of the academy, where the matron was superintending the work of several of the hired girls.

"Oh, Mrs. Green, come quick!" he gasped, as he caught the lady by the arm.

"What is it, Tom?"

"It's poor Peleg! They say he's got a fit! He wants some soothing syrup, or something!"

"Well, I never!" ejaculated Mrs. Green. "A fit! Poor man! Shall I ring for the doctor?"

"Perhaps you had better ring for two doctors, or else come and see if you can help him."

"I'll do what I can," answered the matron, and ran to get some medicine from a chest. "I know what it is," she added. "It's indigestion. He ate four ears of green corn for dinner and four for supper,—and it was very green at that."

"Then he will surely want Mrs. Green to help him," murmured Tom.

Off hurried the matron with some medicine and Tom at her heels.

In the meantime the boys had marched poor Peleg close to the fire.

"Now, steady," cried Sam. "Don't let him fall into the flames and singe his hair."

"Let us warm his feet for him," cried a cadet. "Take off his shoes and stockings!"

"Hi, don't you do nuthin' of the kind," cried Peleg Snuggers, in new alarm. "My feet are warm enough!"

But there was no help for it, and in a twinkling off came his shoes and his socks followed.

"I ain't a-goin' to have my feet warmed!" groaned the utility man. "You are worse nor heathens! Lemme go!"

He struggled violently, but the cadets placed him on the grass and sat on him. Then one, who had run down to the ice-house for a piece of ice, came up.

"Here's a red-hot poker," he said. "Peleg, don't you want your initials branded on your feet?"

"No! no! Oh, help! somebody, help!" yelled the utility man.

"Be careful, or he may get a spasm," whispered Dick, who was looking on without taking part.

"Oh, he's all right," returned the cadet with the ice. "Wait till I brand a P on one foot and an S on the other!" And he drew the ice across the sole of one foot as he spoke.

The poor utility man thought it was a red-hot poker and gave a yell which would have done credit to a South Sea savage. He squirmed and fought, and in the midst of the melee Mrs. Green and Tom arrived.

"There he is," said Tom. "He certainly must have a fit."

"Poor Peleg!" cried Mrs. Green. "Here, my dear, take this. It will do you good." And she held out the bottle of medicine she had brought. "Take about a big spoonful."

"Hurrah, Mrs. Green to the rescue!" shouted Sam. "Come, Peleg, don't be backward about coming forward."

"What is this, Mrs. Green?" asked the astonished man-of-all-work, as he suddenly sat up.

"It's for your cramps, or fits, or whatever you've got, Peleg."

"Cramps, or fits? I ain't got no cramps or fits! Are you crazy, Mrs. Green?"

"Oh, Peleg, don't act so! You certainly have cramps, or indigestion. Come, take the medicine!"

"That fer your medicine!" roared the angry man-of-all-work, and flung the bottle into the bonfire.

"Oh, that medicine!" shrieked the matron. "And I made it myself, too!"

"It's them pesky boys, Mrs. Green! They be a-tormenting the life out of me."

"The boys?" The matron stopped short in wonder.

"Yes, mum. They've stolen my shoes and socks, and they started to brand me with a red-hot poker. I ain't got no fits, nur cramps, nur nuthin', I ain't!"

"Well, I declare!" burst out the thoroughly angry matron. "Tom Rover, come here!"

"Thank you, Mrs. Green, I'll come day after to-morrow!" murmured Tom, as he kept at a safe distance.

"Well, I guess you are all in this together," went on Mrs. Green, looking at the crowd of cadets. "It's your last night and I suppose you will tear the academy down over our ears."

"Why, Mrs. Green, we never do anything wrong," said Sam, reproachfully.

"Oh, no, of course not," was the sarcastic answer. "I'll be thankful to find myself alive after you are all gone." And with this reply the matron bounced off into the kitchen, where she slammed the door after her.

"Here are your shoes, Peleg," said George Granbury, as he handed them over.

"I want my socks first."

"Here you are," came from Larry Colby. As Larry's term as major was now over he was inclined to be as full of fun as anybody.

Peleg took his socks and his shoes and started to put on the former.

"Hullo, what's this!" he cried, and shook one foot violently. "What's in that sock! A grasshopper, I declare! Larry Colby, did you do that?"

"Why, Peleg, you know I never play any jokes," answered the ex-major, innocently.

"Don't I, though! But never mind." The general-utility man started to put on the other sock. "If you think—Great snakes, what's this? Oh, my foot! A hop-toad! Beastly!" And Peleg flung the toad at Larry. The ex-major dodged and the animal struck William Philander Tubbs full in the face.

"Oh, ah—what do you—ah—mean by such actions!" stormed the aristocratic cadet. "I shall report this."

"Hurrah, Tubby has gone into the frog-raising business," shouted Tom, merrily.

21

"I shan't put nuthin' on here," went on Peleg Snuggers, and watching his chance, he ran off at top speed, with his shoes in one hand and his socks in the other.

CHAPTER VIII
GOOD-BYE TO PUTNAM HALL

"Now, Songbird, give us one of your best poetical effusions," came from Dick Rover, after the excitement had died down a little. "We haven't heard a word out of you for fourteen minutes and a quarter."

"Yes, Songbird, turn on the poetry spigot and let her flow," put in Tom.

"Give us something on old schooldays," came from another cadet.

"Put in a touch of last farewells," added another.

"Don't forget to speak of the moon and fond memories."

"Or, shall we ever forget?"

"Or, camping on the old camp-ground, Songbird."

"And of all things, mention the soup we had last Thursday. No piece of poetry would be complete without that soup."

"Who's making up poetry about soup?" roared Songbird Powell. But then he grew calmer. "All right, fellows, here goes." And he started:

"Of all the days to mem'ry dear,
The dearest days are those spent here,
  When we—"

"That's a libel!" interrupted Tom. "Captain Putnam's rates are no higher than the rates of other first-class academies. I move we cut that verse out, Songbird."

"I didn't mean the cost of the days spent here."

"You can't spend anything here," put in George Granbury. "You have to go to Cedarville to do your shopping."

"I'll make a fresh start," came from Powell, and he warbled:

"Old Putnam Hall I do adore,
And love the place as ne'er before,
The campus, boathouse, fishing pier—
The roads that run from far and near—
Each classroom is a hallowed spot,
Though many lessons are forgot!
The dormitories, bright and clean—
No better rooms were ever seen!
The mess-room, where we gathered oft—"

"To eat our eggs both hard and soft!"

finished up Tom, and then went on:

"The prison wherein I was cast,
And thought that day would be my last,
The teachers sweet and the teachers sour,
And the feasts we held at the midnight hour,
The games of ball we lost and won,
And the jubilees! What lots of fun!
And then the skating on the ice—"

"When we broke in, 'twas not so nice:"

interrupted George Granbury, referring to a calamity the particulars of which have already been related in "The Rover Boys in the Mountains." And then Songbird Powell took up the strain once more:

"I love each corner and each nook,
I love the lake and love the brook,
I love the cedars waving high—"

"And love the dinners with mince pie,"

interrupted Tom once more, and continued:

"In fact, I love it one and all,
There is no spot like Putnam Hall!"
And then, with one accord, all standing around joined in the academy cheer:
"Zip, boom, bang! Ding, dong! Ding, dong! Bang! Hurrah for Putnam Hall!" Then the fire was stirred up, more boxes and barrels piled on top, and the cadets danced around more wildly than ever. They were allowed to keep up the fun until midnight, when all were so tired that further sport was out of the question, and all went sound asleep.

Bright and early the next morning the cadets assembled for their last breakfast in the mess-room. The parade was dispensed with, for some had to leave by the early boat on the lake in order to make the proper connections. Many were the handshakings and the kind words of farewell. Some of the students had graduated and were not to come back. Of these a few were bound for college, while others were going into various lines of business.

"We shall never forget our days at Putnam .Hall!" said more than one.

"And I shall never forget you, boys," answered Captain Putnam. "I wish all of you the best of success in life."

It was not until ten o'clock that the three Rover boys left for Cedarville in the big school stage. As was usual, Peleg Snuggers drove the turnout, which was filled to overflowing with cadets. Behind the stage came a big wagon, heavily loaded with trunks and boxes.

"Now, young gents, no cutting up," pleaded the general-utility man.
"The hosses won't stand it, nowhow!"

"That's an old scare, Peleg," replied Tom. He had a tin horn and gave a loud blast. "That will let folks know we are coming." And then a dozen other horns sounded out, while some of the cadets began to sing.

A few minutes after reaching the steamboat dock at the village, which, as my old readers know, was located on the shore of Cayuga Lake, the *Golden Star* came along and made her usual landing. The boat looked familiar to them and they gave the captain a rousing greeting.

Over a dozen pupils were to make the trip to Ithaca at the foot of the lake. There the Rovers would get aboard a train which would take them to Oak Run, the nearest railroad station to their home.

"The *Golden Star* looks like an old friend," remarked Dick, when they were seated on the front, upper deck, enjoying the refreshing breeze that was blowing.'

"I am never on this boat but what I think of our first meeting with Dan Baxter and with Dora Stanhope and Nellie and Grace Laning," came from Tom. "What an enemy Dan Baxter has been from that time on!"

"And what a pile of things have happened since that time!" was Sam's comment. "By the way, it is strange that none of us have heard from any of those girls lately. They ought to be coming east from California by this time."

"I wish they were home," went on Tom. "I'd like to propose something."

"Maybe you'd like to propose to Nellie," put in his younger brother, slyly.

"No sooner than you'd propose to Grace," was Tom's prompt answer, which made Sam blush. "Dick," he went on, "wouldn't it be great if we could get the girls and Mrs. Stanhope to take that trip with us on the houseboat?"

"That would certainly be immense," cried the eldest Rover, enthusiastically. "Why didn't we think of it before? We might have written to them about it."

"Is it too late to write now?" asked Sam. "Or, maybe we can telegraph."

"Perhaps Mrs. Laning wants her girls at home now," said Dick, slowly. "They have been away a long time, remember."

"Perhaps Mrs. Laning might go along. We could have a jolly time of it with six or seven boys and perhaps the same number of girls and ladies."

The idea of having the girls along interested the three Rovers greatly and they talked of practically nothing else during the trip on Cayuga Lake.

23

Ithaca reached, they bid farewell to the last of their school chums, who were to depart in various directions, and then made their way to one of the hotels for dinner.

"There they are, mamma!" they heard a well-known voice exclaim. "Oh, how glad I am that we didn't miss them!" And the next moment Dora Stanhope rushed up, followed by Nellie and Grace Laning and Mrs. Stanhope.

"Well, of all things!" ejaculated Dick, as he shook hands warmly. "Where did you drop from?"

"We were talking about you during the trip from Cedarville," said Tom, as he too shook hands all around, followed by Sam.

"We were wondering why you hadn't written," added Sam.

"We were going to surprise you," answered Grace. "We expected to get home yesterday and visit the academy. But there was a breakdown on the line and our train was delayed and that made us miss a connection."

"We thought sure we'd miss you," said Nellie. "It made us feel awfully."

"Have you dined yet?" asked Dick.

"No."

"Then you must all come and take dinner with us. We want to hear all you've got to tell."

"And we want to hear what you've got to tell too," said Dora, with a merry laugh. She was looking straight into Dick's eyes. "Have you had a good time at the Hall?"

"Yes, but we had a better time at the encampment."

"I heard you met some very nice young ladies up there," went on Dora.

"Who wrote to you about that, Dora?"

"Oh, never mind; I heard it, and that's enough."

"Well, we did meet some nice young ladies."

"Oh!" And Dora turned away for a moment. They were on their way to the dining room and the others were temporarily out of hearing.

"But I didn't meet anybody half as nice as you!" went on Dick, in a low tone of voice, and caught her hand.

"Oh, Dick!" She said this with a toss of her head, but smiled, nevertheless.

"It's true, Dora. I wished you were there more than once. I would have written more, only we had a whole lot of trouble with our enemies."

"And you really did think of me?"

"I did—nearly every day. I suppose you forgot all about me, and that's why you didn't write."

"Dick Rover, you know better than that!"

"I suppose you met some stunning Californian that owns a gold mine and he claimed all of your attention."

"I did meet one rich young man, and—and he proposed to me," faltered Dora.

"Oh, Dora!" And now Dick's heart seemed to stop beating. "And you—you didn't accept him, did you?"

"Would you care if I did?" she whispered. "Dora!" he answered, half fiercely.

"Well, I told him I didn't want him, so there," said Dora, hurriedly. "I told him that I wanted to marry somebody that lived in the East, and that I—I—"

"And that you had the young man picked out? Why didn't you tell him that, Dora? You know—"

"Hi, you folks!" came in a cry from Tom. "What are you steering for the smoking room for? We are bound for the dining room."

"Well, I never!" murmured Dora. "Dick, we had better watch out where we are going."

"That's right." They turned toward the dining room. "Dora, you know, as I was saying, that—"

"Dick Rover, I thought we were going to dinner! Just see the folks! What a crowd! You musn't talk like that here."

"Yes, that's true, but—"

"You really must mind, Dick." She gave him a bright smile. "I—I—guess I understand you!"

And then all went in to dinner.

CHAPTER IX

THE ROVER BOYS AT HOME

There was a great deal to tell on all sides, and the dinner lasted over an hour. The Stanhopes and the Lanings had had a grand time while at Santa Barbara and the widow was much improved in health, so much so, in fact, that she was now practically a well woman. Those who had been in the Far West listened with interest to the boys' doings at the Hall and during the encampment, and were amazed to think that Dan Baxter and his father had turned up once more, and that Arnold Baxter was trying to turn over a new leaf.

"I do not believe Dan will ever turn over a new leaf," said Dora. "He is a thoroughly bad young man."

"Let us hope that he does," said her mother. "I do not wish to see anybody throw himself away as that young man is doing."

"After this you will have to watch out for this Lew Flapp as well as for Dan Baxter," said Nellie. "Both appear to be painted with the same brush."

During the dinner the houseboat project was broached, and the boys spoke of what a fine time they expected to have on the Ohio, and perhaps on the Mississippi.

"And we would like all of you to go with us," said Dick.

"With you!" exclaimed Mrs. Stanhope.

"Oh, mamma, what a delightful trip it would be!" exclaimed Dora.

"And we would like your mother to go too," went on Tom, to Nellie and Grace.

"Oh, if mamma would only go!" cried Grace. "I am sure it would do her a great deal of good. She goes away from home so little."

The matter was talked over until it was time for the two parties to separate, and the Rovers promised to write more particulars in a few days,—as soon as they knew more about the houseboat and how it was to be run, and what sort of sleeping accommodations it afforded.

The boys saw the Stanhopes and the Lanings on the boat bound up the lake and then almost ran to the depot to catch their train. It came in directly, and in half a minute more they were being whirled away in the direction of Oak Run.

"There is no use of talking, those girls are just all right," said Sam, bluntly. "I never met a nicer lot in my life."

"I guess Dick thinks one of them is all right," said Tom, with a grin. "Although I don't see why you were steering her into the smoking room," he added, to his big brother. "Were you going to teach her to smoke cigarettes?"

"Oh, say, Tom, let up," grumbled Dick. "You paid about as much attention to Nellie as I did to Dora."

"Anyway, I didn't steer her to the smoking room."

"No, but while you were talking to her I saw you put five spoonfuls of sugar in her coffee for her," returned Dick. "Maybe you didn't think she was sweet enough for you, eh?"

At this Tom reddened, while Sam set up a roar.

"He's got you, Tom!" cried the youngest Rover. "Better cry quits and talk about something else. We all like those girls amazingly, and that's the end of it;" and then the subject was changed.

It was almost dark when Oak Run was reached. Here a carriage, driven by Jack Ness, the Rovers' hired man, was in waiting for them.

"Hullo, Jack!" cried Tom. "All well at home?"

"Very well, Master Tom," was the answer. "And how are you, and how is Master Dick and Master Sam?"

"All O. K. and top side up, Jack," said Sam.

They were soon in the carriage, and then the hired man whipped up the team and away they sped across Swift River, through the village of Dexter's Corners, and then along the highway leading to the farm.

"I see the lights of home!" sang out Sam, as they made the last turn. "I can tell you, it makes a fellow feel good, doesn't it?"

"It's a true saying that there is no place like home," returned Dick. "Here we are!"

The carriage made a turn around a clump of trees and then dashed up to the piazza. From the house rushed several people.

"Here we are, father!" sang out Dick. "How are you, Uncle Randolph, and how are you, Aunt Martha?"

"Dick!" cried Mr. Anderson Rover, and embraced his oldest son. "And Tom and Sam! I am glad to see you looking so well!"

"My boys!" murmured their aunt, as of old, and gave each a sounding kiss.

"Getting to be big young men," was their uncle's comment. "They won't be boys much longer."

"I'm going to stay a boy all my life, Uncle Randolph," answered Tom, promptly. "By the way," he went on, with a merry twinkle in his eye, "how is scientific farming getting on?"

"Splendidly, Thomas, splendidly."

"Not losing money any more, then?"

"Well—er—I have lost a little, just a little, this summer. But next summer I expect grand results."

"Going to grow a new kind of turnip?"

"No I—"

"Or maybe it's a squash this time, uncle."

"No, I am trying—"

"Or a parsnip. I have heard there is a great call for parsnips in New Zealand. The natives use them for dyeing—"

"Thomas!" interrupted his father, sternly. "Please don't start to joke so early. To-morrow will do."

"All right, I'll subside," answered Tom. "But really, do you know, I'm bubbling all over, like an uncorked soda-water bottle."

"Don't you feel hungry?"

"Hungry! Just you try me and see."

"I made a big cherry pie for you, Tom," said his aunt. "I know you like it."

"Oh, Aunt Martha, that's worth an extra hug." He gave it to her. "Your pie can't be beat!"

"And I've got some fried chicken. Dick likes that."

"And I like it, too," said Sam.

"Yes, I know it, Sam. But I made some spice cakes too—"

"Oh, aunt, just my weakness!" cried the youngest Rover. "There's another kiss for you, and another! You're the best aunt a boy ever had!"

They were soon washed up and sitting down to the table. Scarcely had they seated themselves than Alexander Pop came in, acting as waiter, something he always did when the boys came home. Alexander, usually called Aleck for short, was a good-natured colored man who had once been employed at Putnam Hall. He had gone to Africa with the Rover boys, as already related in "The Rover Boys in the Jungle," and had been with them on numerous other trips. He was now employed steadily in the Rover household.

"Howde do, gen'men?" he said, with a broad grin on his coal-black face.

"Aleck!" all three cried together; "how are you?"

"Fust-rate, thank yo'. Yo' am looking right smart, too," went on the colored man. And then he began to serve them with the best the place afforded. He loved dearly to talk, but thought the present no time for so doing.

It was a happy family gathering, and all remained at the table a long time, the boys telling their different tales from beginning to end. Mr. Anderson Rover was much interested in what they had to say about the Baxters and Lew Flapp.

"You must be careful," said he. "Arnold Baxter can do you no more harm, but the others will be worse than snakes in the grass."

"We'll watch out," answered Dick, and then he and the others asked about the houseboat which had been taken for debt and how soon they could use the craft.

"You may use the houseboat as soon as you please," said Randolph Rover. "But you must promise your father and Aunt Martha and me not to get into mischief."

"How could we get into mischief with a houseboat?" questioned Tom. "Why, we just intend to knock around and take it easy all summer."

"The rest ought to do all of you a power of good," came from his father. "I declare, it seems to me you have been on the jump ever since you first went to Putnam Hall."

"Where is the houseboat now?"

"Tied up at the village of Steelville, not very far from Pittsburg. As I wrote to you, she is under the command of Captain Starr. He knows the Ohio and the Mississippi thoroughly and will take you wherever you wish to go."

"Well, we want to stay home a few days first, and make all of our arrangements," said Dick; and so it was decided.

CHAPTER X
A SCENE IN A CEMETERY

"Hurrah, Fred Garrison says he will go with us!" cried Sam, two days later. "I have just received a telegram from him. He says he will come on to-morrow."

"And here is word from Songbird Powell," put in Dick. "He will go, too. He is to meet us at Pittsburg, any time I say."

"And Hans Mueller will go," said Tom. "That makes three of our friends to start with. I hope the Lanings and the Stanhopes go."

"So do I," answered Dick, who could not get that talk with Dora in the hallway of the hotel out of his head.

Sam was anxious to meet Fred Garrison, and on the following afternoon drove down to the railroad station at Oak Run to greet his chum.

The train was late, and after finding this out Sam took a walk around the village to see what changes had been made during the past few months. But Oak Run was a slow place and he look in vain for improvements.

"Guess I'll have my hair cut while I am here," he said to himself, and started to enter the only barber shop of which the railroad village boasted.

As he pushed open the door a young fellow got out of one of the chairs and paid the barber what was coming to him. Then he reached for his hat and started to leave.

"Lew Flapp!" ejaculated Sam. "Is it possible?"

The bully of Putnam Hall whirled around and gave a start. He had not dreamed of meeting one of the Rovers.

"What—er—what do you want?" he stammered, not knowing what to say.

"Where did you come from, Flapp?"

"That's my business."

"It was a fine trick you played on us while we were on the march back to Putnam Hall."

"Trick? I haven't played any trick on you," answered Lew Flapp, loftily, as he began to regain his self-possession.

"You know well enough that you robbed that jewelry shop and then tried to lay the blame on me and my brothers."

"Rover, you are talking in riddles."

"No, I'm not; I'm telling the strict truth."

"Bah!" Lew Flapp shoved forward. "Let me pass."

"Not just yet." Sam placed himself in front of the barber shop door.

"What's the row?" put in the barber, who happened to be the only other person in the shop.

"This fellow is a thief, Mr. Gregg."

"You don't say!" cried Lemuel Gregg. "Who did he rob?"

"He robbed a jewelry shop up near Putnam Hall and then he laid the blame on my brothers and me."

"That was a mean thing to do."

"It is false!" roared Lew Flapp. "Get out of my way, or it will be the worse for you!"

"I'm not afraid of you, Flapp," responded Sam, sturdily. "Mr. Gregg, will you help me to make him a prisoner?"

"Are you certain of what you are doing?" questioned the barber, nervously. "I don't want to get into trouble over this. I once cut off a man's beard by mistake and had to pay twenty-two dollars damages."

"I know exactly what I am doing. Help me to make him a prisoner and you shall be well rewarded."

At the promise of a reward Lemuel Gregg became interested. He knew that the Rovers were well-to-do and could readily pay him handsomely for his services.

"You—you had better stay here, young man," he said, to Lew Flapp. "If you are innocent it won't hurt you. We'll have the squire look into this case."

"I won't stay!" roared the bully, and making a sudden leap at Sam he hurled the youngest Rover to one side and tried to bolt through the door.

"No, you don't!" came from the barber, and leaping to the front he caught Lew Flapp by the end of the coat and held him.

"Let go!"

"I won't!"

"Then take that!" And the next instant Lew Flapp hit the barber a telling blow in the nose which made the blood spurt from that member. Then Flapp dove for the door, pulled it open, and sped up the street with all speed.

"Oh, my nose! He has smashed it to jelly!" groaned the barber, as he rushed to the sink for some water.

Sam had been thrown against a barber chair so forcibly that for the moment the wind was knocked completely out of him. By the time he was able to stand up, Flapp was out of the building.

"We must catch him!" he cried. "Come on!"

"Catch him yourself," growled Lemuel Gregg, "I ain't going to stand the risk of being killed. He's a reg'lar tiger, he is!" And he began to bathe his nose at the sink.

Lew Flapp was running towards the railroad, but as soon as he saw that Sam was on his track he made several turns, finally taking to a side road which led to the Oak Run Cemetery. Here he saw there were numerous bushes and cedar trees, and thought he could hide or double on his trail without discovery.

But he forgot one thing—that Sam was a splendid runner and good of wind as well as limb. Try his best, he could not shake the youngest Rover off.

"The fool!" muttered the bully to himself. "Why don't he give it up?"

Flapp looked about him for a club, but none was at hand. Then he picked up a stone and taking aim, hurled it at Sam. The missile struck the youngest Rover in the shoulder, causing considerable pain.

"I reckon two can play at that game," murmured Sam, and he too caught up a stone and launched it forth. It landed in the middle of Lew Flapp's back and caused the bully to utter a loud cry of anguish.

"Stop, Flapp! I am bound to catch you sooner or later!" cried Sam.

"You come closer and I'll fix you!" growled the bully. "I'll hammer the life out of you!"

"You've got to spell able first," answered Sam.

The cemetery gained, Lew Flapp ran along one of the paths leading to the rear. Along this path were a number of good-sized sticks. He picked up one of these, and a few seconds later Sam did likewise.

Near the rear of the cemetery was a new receiving vault, which had just been donated to the cemetery association by the widow of a rich stockholder who had died the year before. The vault was of stone, with a heavy iron door that shut with a catch and a lock.

Making a turn that hid him from Sam's view for the moment, Lew Flapp espied the vault, standing with the door partly open.

"He won't look for me in there," reasoned the bully, and slipped into the place with all possible alacrity. Once inside, he crouched in a dark corner behind the door and waited.

Sam, making the turn at just the right instant, saw Flapp disappearing into the vault. Without stopping he ran forward and closed the iron door, allowing the heavy catch to slip into place.

"Now, Lew Flapp, I guess I've got you!" he called out, after he was certain the door was secure.

To this the bully made no answer, but it is more than likely his heart sank within him.

"Do you hear me, Flapp? You needn't pretend you are not in there, for I saw you go in."

Still Lew Flapp made no answer.

"Do you want me to go away and leave you locked in the vault?" continued Sam. "It would be a beautiful place in which to die of starvation."

"Let me out!" came from the bully, and now he got up and showed his face at the small grating near the top of the door. "Let me out, Rover, that's a good fellow."

"Then you don't want to die of starvation just yet?"

"You wouldn't dare to leave me here, you know you wouldn't!"

"Why not? Don't you deserve it, after the trick you played on Dick and Tom and me?"

"I tell you it's all a mistake. Let me out and I will explain everything," went on Flapp, who was now thoroughly alarmed.

"I'll let you out—after I have summoned the town constable."

"Don't have me locked up, I beg of you, Sam. Give me a chance," pleaded the bully.

"You don't deserve any chance. You tried to send me and my brothers to prison, and you have got to suffer for it."

"Then you won't let me out?"

"No."

"I'll pay you well for it."

"You haven't got money enough to pay me, Flapp, and you know it."

"If you have me locked up I'll say you helped me in that robbery."

"Ah, so you admit you did it," cried Sam, triumphantly.

"No, I admit nothing," growled the bully.

"Good-bye, then."

"Where are you going?"

"I am going after the cemetery keeper and the constable," answered Sam, and walked off without another word.

CHAPTER XI

ATTACKED FROM BEHIND

Lew Flapp watched Sam's departure with much anxiety. As my old readers know, he was a coward at heart, and the thought of being put under arrest for the robbery of Aaron Fairchild's shop made him quake in every limb.

"I must get out of here, I really must," he told himself, over and over again.

He shook the door violently, but it refused to budge. Then he tried to reach the catch by putting his hand through the grating, but found it was out of his reach.

"It's a regular prison cell!" he groaned. "What a fool I was to come in here!"

He tried to reach the catch by using his stick, but that was also a failure.

"Wonder if I can't find a bit of wire, or something?" he mused, and struck a match he had in his pocket.

Now it chanced that the widow who had given the new vault to the cemetery association had a horror of allowing supposed dead folks to be buried alive. As a consequence she had had the vault furnished with an electric button which opened the door from the inside. It had been stipulated that a light should be placed close to the button, but as yet this was not in place.

By the light of the match Lew Flapp saw the button, and these words over it:

To Open the Door and Ring the Bell Push This Button.

"Good! that just suits me," he chuckled to himself, but immediately had something of a chill, thinking that the button might not yet be fixed to work.

With nervous fingers he pushed upon the object. There was a slight click, and he saw the big iron door of the vault spring ajar.

"The trick is done, and I am free!" he murmured, and sprang to the door. But here he paused again, to gaze through the grating. Sam was out of sight and not another soul could be seen. The coast was clear.

"Now good-bye to Oak Run," he muttered to himself. "I was a fool to come here in the first place, even to meet that Dan Baxter!"

In a moment more he was out of the vault and running to the rear of the cemetery as fast as his legs would carry him.

In the meantime Sam made his way as quickly as possible to a house situated at the front corner of the cemetery, where the keeper of the place resided.

A knock on the door brought the keeper's daughter. She knew Sam and smiled.

"What can I do for you, Sam?" she asked.

"Where is your father, Jennie?"

"He just went down to the village to buy a new spade."

"Oh, pshaw! that's too bad."

"What is the matter? I hope you're not going to have a funeral in your family."

"No funeral in this, Jennie. I met a thief in Oak Run and tried to have him arrested. He ran into the cemetery and hid in the new vault and I locked the door on him. Now I want your father or somebody else to help me take him to the lock-up."

"A thief! What did he steal?"

"Some jewelry. It's a long story. Do you know where I can find somebody else?"

"Jack Sooker is working over to the other end of the cemetery—cutting down an old tree. You might get him."

"Where?"

"I'll show you."

Jennie ran to get her hat. She was just putting it on when a bell began to ring in the hall of the cottage.

"Gracious me!" gasped the girl.

"What's the matter now?"

"That's the bell to the new vault."

"I don't understand."

"There is an electric button in the vault. When you push it, it unlocks the door and rings this bell. It was put there in case somebody was in the vault in a trance and came to life again."

"What!" ejaculated Sam. "Then that rascal must have pushed the button and opened the door from the inside."

"Yes."

"I'm off. He is not going to escape if I can help it." And so speaking, the youngest Rover dashed off the porch of the cottage and in the direction from whence he had come.

It did not take him long to reach the new vault and a glance through the open doorway showed him that his bird had flown.

"What a dunce I was not to think of that electric button!" he mused. "I knew Mrs. Singleton had stipulated it should be put in. She has a perfect horror of being buried alive."

Sam looked around in all directions, but could see nothing of Lew Flapp.

But not far away was a pile of loose dirt and in this he saw some fresh tracks, pointing to the rear of the cemetery.

"That's his course," he thought, and set off in that direction. He still carried the stick he had picked up and vowed that Lew Flapp should not get away so easily again.

The end of the cemetery bordered on the Swift River, a stream which has already figured in these stories of the Rover boys. It was a rocky, swift-flowing watercourse, and the bank at the end of the burying ground was fully ten feet high.

"Perhaps he crossed the river," thought the youngest Rover. "But he couldn't do that very well unless he had a boat and then he would run the risk of being dashed on the rocks."

The edge of the river reached, Sam looked around on all sides of him. Lew Flapp was still nowhere to be seen.

"I've missed him," thought Sam. "What next?"

As the youngest Rover stood meditating, a figure stole from behind some bushes which were close at hand. The figure was that of Lew Flapp, who had been on the point of turning back when he had seen Sam coming.

"He will raise an alarm as soon as he sees me," reasoned the bully. "Oh, if only I could get him out of my way!"

He gazed at the youngest Rover and when he saw how close to the water's edge Sam was standing, a sudden thought came into his mind. As silently as a wild beast stealing on its prey, he crept up to Sam.

"There! how do like that, Sam Rover!" he cried, triumphantly, and gave the youngest Rover a shove which sent him over the bank and into the rocky stream below.

Sam gave out one yell and then, with a loud splash, sank beneath the surface.

Lew Flapp gazed for a second in the direction, wondering when Sam would reappear. But then a new fear took possession of him and off he ran, this time harder than ever.

His course was along the river bank for a distance of a hundred yards, and then he came out on a road leading to a small place called Hacknack.

"To Hacknack!" he muttered, after reading a signboard. "That's the place I'm looking for. One mile, eh? Well, I had better lose no time in getting there."

The bully was a fair walker and now fear lent speed to his limbs, and in less than fifteen minutes he reached the hamlet named. He gazed around and presently located a small cottage standing near the edge of a sandpit.

"That must be the cottage," he told himself, and walking to it he rapped on the door four times in succession and then four times again.

There was a stir within and then an old woman, bent with age and with a wicked look in her sharp, yellowish eyes, came to answer his summons.

"Is this Mother Matterson's place?" he asked.

"Yes, I'm Mother Matterson," squeaked the old woman. "Who are you and what do you want?"

"My name is Lew Flapp. I'm looking for a fellow called Si Silvers," he added, for that was the name Dan Baxter had assumed for the time being.

"It's all right, old woman; tell him to come in," said a voice from inside the cottage, and Lew Flapp entered the house. Immediately the old woman closed the door after him and barred it.

CHAPTER XII
FLAPP AND BAXTER PLOT MISCHIEF

The cottage which Mother Matterson occupied was a much dilapidated one of a story and a half, containing three rooms and a loft. Some of the windows were broken out and the chimney was sadly in need of repair.

Many were the rumors afloat concerning this old woman. Some said she was little short of being a witch, while others had it that she was in league with tramps who had stolen things for miles around. But so far, if guilty, she had escaped the penalty of the law.

"So you've come at last," went on the person in the cottage, as Lew Flapp came in, and a moment later Dan Baxter came into view. He was tall and lanky as of old, with a sour look on his face and several scars which made him particularly repulsive. "I had almost given you up."

"I've had my own troubles getting here," answered Flapp. "At first I couldn't locate Hacknack and then I had the misfortune to fall in with Sam Rover"

"Sam Rover! Is he on your track now?"

"I rather guess not," and the bully of Putnam Hall gave a short laugh. "He has gone swimming for his health."

"What do you mean?"

"I'll tell you," answered Lew Flapp, and in a rapid manner he related all that had occurred since he had met Sam in the Oak Run barber shop.

"Well, all I can say is, that you are a lucky dog," came from Dan Baxter, at the conclusion of the recital. "You can thank your stars that you are not at this moment in the Oak Run lock-up."

"I shouldn't have run any risk at all if it hadn't been for you," growled Flapp.

"Oh, don't come any such game on me, Flapp. I can read you like a book. You know you don't dare to go home—after that trip-up at White Corners. Your old man would just about kill you—and you'd be locked up in the bargain."

At these words Lew Flapp winced, for he knew that Dan Baxter spoke the truth. He was afraid to go home, and had come to Hacknack simply because he knew not where else to go and because Baxter had promised him some money. The amount he had realized on the sale of the stolen jewelry had been spent.

"See here, what's the use of talking that way?" he grumbled. "I didn't come here to get a lecture."

"I'm not lecturing you," came hastily from Dan Baxter. "I'm merely telling you things for your own good, Flapp. I want you to pull with me. I know we'll get along swimmingly."

"You said you'd let me have some money."

"And I'll keep my word."

"I need at least fifty dollars."

"You'll need more than that, Flapp. You've got to stay away from home until this matter blows over, or until your old man patches things up with that Aaron Fairchild and the White Corners authorities. I've got a plan, if you care to listen to it."

"Sure, I'll listen—if you'll only let me have that money."

"I'll let you have all you want—providing you'll agree to help me."

32

"Well, what is your plan? But first tell me, how about this woman?" And Flapp nodded his head toward Mother Matterson.

"Don't you worry about her," grinned Dan Baxter. "I've got her fixed. She won't squeal."

"Then go ahead."

"As I said before, the best thing you can do is to stay away from home until this unpleasantness blows over. Write to your father and tell him it is all a mistake, and that you are not guilty but that you can't prove it. Ask him to square the thing with Aaron Fairchild and the others, and tell him you are going on an ocean trip and won't be back until you know you are safe. Then you come with me, and we'll have a jolly good time, besides squaring up matters with the Rovers."

"Where are you going and how are you going to square matters with them?"

"I've learned a thing or two since I came here. At first I was going to try to fix them while they were at home, but now I've learned that they are going away on a houseboat trip on the Ohio and the Mississippi. I propose to follow them and give them more than they want the first opportunity that presents itself."

"You are certain about this houseboat trip?"

"I am."

"And who is going?"

"The three Rover boys and some of their school chums."

"Humph! I'd like to get square with the whole crowd!" muttered Lew Flapp. "I'd like to sink them in the middle of the Ohio River!"

"We'll square up, don't you worry," answered Dan Baxter. "I'm not forgetting all they've done against me in the past. If I had the chance I'd wring the neck of every one of them," he added, fiercely.

"I don't think it is safe to stay around here any longer," said Lew Flapp, after a pause. "Somebody may spot us both."

"I'm not going to stay any longer. We can get out on the night train. By the way, supposing Sam Rover doesn't get out of the river."

"What do you mean?" questioned Flapp, with a shiver, although he knew well enough.

"Maybe Sam Rover was drowned."

"Oh, don't say that!"

"Bah! Don't be chicken-hearted, Flapp."

"I—I—didn't mean to—to—kill him."

"I know you didn't. Just the same that is a dangerous river. The current is swift and it's full of rocks."

"You're making me feel very uncomfortable."

"Oh, don't worry, Those Rover boys are like cats—each has nine lives. Sam Rover will be hot-footed after you before you know it."

"Have you got that money with you, Baxter?"

"To be sure I have. I never travel without a wad."

"Then let me have some."

"You won't need it, if we are to travel together."

"We may become separated," urged Lew Flapp. He did not altogether trust his companion.

"Well, I reckon that's so, too. I'll let you have twenty-five dollars. When that's gone you can come to me for more. But remember one thing: you've got to help me to down the Rovers."

"I'll help you to do that. But—but—"

"But what?"

"We mustn't go too far."

"Oh, you leave that to me. You've heard how they treated my father, haven't you?"

"They say Dick Rover was kind to him."

33

"Bah! That's a fairy story."

"But your father says the same—so I have been told."

"The old man is out of his head—on account of that fire. When he gets clear-headed again he won't think Dick Rover—or any of the Rovers, for the matter of that—is his friend."

There was another pause.

"Where do you propose to go to?"

"Philadelphia, on a little business first, and then to Pittsburg, and to that place where they have their houseboat."

"And after that?"

"I'm going to be guided by circumstances. But you can rest assured of one thing, Flapp—I'll make those Rover boys wish they had never undertaken this trip."

Dan Baxter brought out a pocketbook well filled with bank bills and counted out five five-dollar bills.

"My, but you're rich!" cried the bully of Putnam Hall.

"Oh, I've got a good bit more than that," was the bragging answer. "I want you to know that once upon a time my father was as rich as the Rovers, and he would be as rich now if it wasn't that they cheated him out of his rights to a gold mine," went on Dan Baxter, bringing up something which has already been fully explained in "The Rover Boys Out West." The claim belonged to the Rovers, but the Baxters would never admit this.

"Did they really cheat him?" questioned Lew Flapp, with interest.

"They certainly did."

"Then why didn't you go to law about it with them?"

"They stole all the evidence, so we couldn't do a thing in law. Do you wonder that I am down on them?"

"No, I don't. If I were you, I'd try to get my rights back."

"I'm going to get them back some day," answered Dan Baxter. "And I am going to square up with all the Rovers, too, mind that!"

CHAPTER XIII
CHIPS AND THE CIRCUS BILLS

It is now time that we return to Sam and find out how he fared after being so unexpectedly hurled into the river by Lew Flapp.

The youngest Rover was taken so completely off his guard that he could, for the moment, do nothing to save himself. Down he went and his yell was cut short by the waters closing over his head.

He was dazed and bewildered and swallowed some of the water almost before he was aware. But then his common-sense returned to him and he struggled to rise to the surface.

As he neared the top, the current carried him against a sharp rock. Instead of clutching this, he hit the rock with his head. The blow almost stunned him, and down he went once more, around the rock and along the river a distance of fully a hundred feet ere he again appeared.

By this time he realized that he was having a battle for his life, and he clutched out wildly for the first thing that came to hand, It was a tree root and by its aid he pulled himself to the surface of the river and gazed around him.

He was under the bank, at a point where the current had washed away a large portion of the soil, exposing to view half of the roots of a tree standing above. To get out of the stream at that spot was an impossibility, and he let himself go once more, when he had regained his breath and felt able to take care of himself.

In a few minutes more Sam reached a point where to climb up the bank was easy, and he lost no time in leaving the river. Once on the bank he squeezed the water out of his garments. He had lost his cap, but spent no time in looking for the head covering.

"Oh, if only I had Lew Flapp here!" he muttered over and over again. But the bully had, as we already know, made good his escape, and Sam found it impossible to get on his track. Soaked to the skin he made his way back through the cemetery.

"Hullo, so you have fallen into the river!" sang out a man who saw him coming. It was Jack Sooker, the fellow mentioned by the cemetery keeper's daughter.

"No, I was pushed in," answered Sam, who knew Sooker fairly well.

"How did it happen, Sam?"

"I was after a rascal I wanted to have locked up. But he shoved me into the river and got away."

"You don't tell me! Where is he now?"

"I don't know."

"That's too bad. Do I know him?"

"No, he is a stranger around these parts."

"A young fellow?"

"Yes, about Dick's age."

"Can't say as I've seen him. What are you going to do about it?"

"I don't know yet. I've got to get some dry clothes first:"

Sam walked up to the cottage at the corner of the cemetery. Jennie, the keeper's daughter, saw him coming and gave a cry at his wet garments.

"Can I dry myself here?" he asked, after he had explained the situation.

"To be sure you can, Sam," she answered, and stirred up the fire in the kitchen stove. "If you wish I'll lend you a suit of my brother Zack's clothes—that is, if you are in a hurry."

"Thanks, I'll borrow the suit. I want to report this; and I'll send the suit back to-morrow."

"You needn't hurry. Zack isn't home just now, so he doesn't need the suit."

The clothes were found, and Sam slipped into a bedchamber of the cottage and made the change. Then, after thanking Jennie once more for her kindness, the youngest Rover set off for Oak Run as fast as he could.

A train was just coming into the depot and the first person to hop off was Fred Garrison.

"Hullo, I thought you'd meet me!" sang out Fred. "How are you?"

"Pretty well, considering," answered Sam, with a quiet smile. "But I've had a whole lot of happenings since I drove down to the depot."

"What's the matter, horse run away?"

"No, I met Lew Flapp."

"Nonsense! Why, what is he doing around here?"

"I give it up, Fred. But he was here and we have had a lively time of it," answered Sam, and told his story.

"Well, I'll be jiggered! What do you propose to do next?"

"I don't know what to do. I might get the village constable to hunt for him, but I don't think it will do any good."

"Why don't you tell your folks first?"

"Yes, I reckon that will be best. Jump in the carriage and I'll drive you over to our home."

Fred had but little to tell out of the ordinary. His folks had wanted him to go to the seashore for the summer, but he had preferred to take the houseboat trip with the Rovers.

"I am sure we shall have a dandy time," he said. "I was on a houseboat trip once, down in Florida, and it was simply great."

"What do you think about the Lanings and the Stanhopes going with us?"

"That will be nice. We certainly ought to have a bang-up time," answered Fred, enthusiastically.

Sam had driven over with the best horse the Rover stable afforded, a magnificent bay, which Anderson Rover had purchased in Albany at a special sale early in the spring. Sam had pleaded to take the steed and his parent had finally consented.

"That's a fine bit of horseflesh you have," observed Fred, as they sped along the level road leading to Valley Brook farm. "I like the manner in which he steps out first-rate."

"Chips is a good horse," answered Sam. "There is only one fault he has."

"And what is that?"

"He is easily frightened at a bit of paper or some other white object in the road."

"That is bad."

The conversation now changed and the boys spoke of the good times ahead. Farm after farm was passed, until they were almost in sight of Valley Brook.

"What a beautiful stretch of country," observed Fred, as he gazed around. "I don't wonder that your uncle settled here while your father was in Africa."

"We used to hate the farm, Tom especially. We thought it was too dead slow for anything. But now we love to come back to it, after being at school or somewhere else."

They were just passing the farm next to that of the Rovers when a man came driving up to them at a rapid gait. He was seated on a buckboard and had behind him a box filled with showbills.

"Visit the circus day after to-morrow! Biggest show on earth for a quarter!" he shouted, and flung a couple of bills at them.

"A circus!" began Fred, when, without warning, Chips made a wild leap that nearly threw him and Sam into the road. Scared by the sight of the showbills the horse made a plunge and then began to run away.

"Whoa, Chips, whoa!" sang out Sam.

"Don't—don't let him get away, Sam!" came from Fred, as he gripped the side of the carriage.

"He shan't get away if I can help it," was the answer, from between Sam's shut teeth. "Whoa, Chips, whoa!" he went on.

But Chips wouldn't whoa, and the sight of another white handbill in the middle of the road caused him to shy to one side. Both boys were unseated, and Sam would have gone to the ground had not Fred held him fast.

"Whoa!" yelled Sam, and now he pulled in tighter than ever on the reins. But on and on went the bay steed, straight through the lane leading to the Rovers' barn.

"He'll smash us up!" gasped Fred.

"Hi! hi!" came from the barnyard and then Dick Rover came into view. His quick eye took in the situation in an instant and he made a grand dash to reach Chips' head. He was successful, and in spite of the steed's efforts to throw him off, held on until at last the bay was brought to a standstill, trembling in every limb and covered with foam.

"How did this happen, Samuel?" asked his uncle, as he too came forward.

"A fellow with circus bills scared him," answered Sam, and he added: "I'd just like to catch that fellow and give him a piece of my mind!"

"And so would I," added Fred.

"Are either of you hurt?"

"No."

"Let us be thankful for that," said Mr. Rover; and then had the horse taken to the stable by Jack Ness.

CHAPTER XIV
FUN AT THE SHOW

As soon as the family were assembled and Fred had been greeted all around, Sam told of what had happened since he had started out to have his hair cut.

"Well, you've had your share of happenings," declared Mrs. Rover. "It is a wonder you are alive to tell of them."

"We ought to go after Lew Flapp," said Dick. "He ought to be arrested by all means."

"Yes, but where are you going to look for him?"

"Perhaps he will take the late train to-night from Oak Run."

"That's an idea," came from Tom. "Let us watch the train."

This was decided upon, and he and Dick, accompanied by their father, went to Oak Run that evening for that purpose. But Lew Flapp and Dan Baxter took the train from a station three miles away, so the quest was unsuccessful.

"I guess he didn't let the grass grow under his feet," said Sam, the next morning. "No doubt he was badly scared."

"What could he have been doing in this neighborhood?" asked Dick.

"I give it up."

During the day Sam got his hair cut and also returned the clothing loaned to him by the cemetery keeper's daughter. While in Oak Run he met the fellow who was distributing circus bills.

"You want to be more careful when distributing bills," said he to the man.

"What's the matter with you?" growled the circus agent.

"You scared my horse yesterday and made him run away."

"Oh, go tumble over yourself," growled the fellow, and turned away.

The manner of the man angered Sam, and likewise angered Tom, who happened to be along.

"Some of those circus chaps think they own the earth," was Tom's comment. "I've a good mind to go to his old circus and have some fun with the outfit."

"Just the thing, Tom! Let us ask the others to go too. I haven't seen a circus in a long time."

"Well, this won't be much to look at. But we may get some fun out of it," added Tom, with a sly wink.

"Yes, there is sure to be fun when you are around," added his younger brother, with a laugh.

When the circus was mentioned at home Dick said he would be glad to go and so did Fred.

"It is Frozzler's Grand Aggregation of Attractions," said Tom, looking over one of the showbills. "The Most Stupendous Exhibition on Earth. Daring bareback riding, trained elephants and a peanut-eating contest, likewise an egg-hunting raffle. All for a quarter, twenty-five cents."

"What is an egg-hunting raffle?" questioned Fred.

"He's fooling you, Fred," answered Sam. "You mustn't believe all Tom says."

"Thus doth mine own flesh go back on me," came from Tom, with an injured look. "Never mind, it is put and carried that we go and see Frozzler's outfit, occupying reserved orchestra chairs, close to the family circle and adjoining the second gallery west."

As soon as it was settled Tom and Sam laid their heads together to have all the fun they could at the circus, "just to get square with that agent," as Sam expressed it.

None of the older folks wanted to go, for which the boys were thankful.

"Say, I'd like to see dat show, Tom," said Aleck Pop, when he got the chance. "Ain't seen no circuses since I was a little boy."

"Then you must go by all means, Aleck. But don't you get too close to the monkey cage."

"Why not, Tom?"

"They might take you for a long-lost brother."

"Yah! yah! Dat's one on me!" Aleck showed his ivories in a broad grin. "Maybe da will take yo' for a long-lost brudder, too—yo' is so full ob monkey shines," and then Tom had to laugh at the sally.

At the proper time the four boys drove over to the circus grounds, taking Aleck Pop with them. Aleck was arrayed in his best, and from his broad expanse of shirt bosom sparkled an imitation diamond which looked like a small electric light.

Tickets were procured for all by Dick, and the boys and the servant pressed their way into the first of the tents, in company with one of the largest crowds ever gathered in that vicinity.

Now, as it happened, Frozzler's Grand Aggregation of Attractions was largely so only in name. Frozzler was himself the man who had given out the showbills, his regular agent having refused to work because his salary had remained unpaid for three weeks. The circus was fast going to pieces.

"Here is where I am going to make a bunch of money," said Frozzler to himself, as he saw the crowd coming in. "This day will put me on my feet again." But he never saw the "bunch" of money in question, for before the show was over a sheriff came along and levied on the receipts, in behalf of several tradespeople and some performers.

The exhibition was held in two tents, one for the wild animals and the other for the ring performance. The wild animals were in exactly eight wagon cages and consisted of a sickly-looking lion, a half-starved tiger, several raccoons, two foxes, a small bear, and about a dozen monkeys. There were also two elephants, one so old he was blind and could hardly stand.

"Well, this is a sell, if ever there was one," murmured Tom, after looking into the various cages.

"I feel like going out to the butcher shop and buying something with which to feed that tiger," answered Dick. "He looks as if he hadn't had a square meal for a week."

"I'm going to give the monkeys some peanuts, that's the best I can do for them," put in Sam.

"If the ring show isn't better than this we are stuck sure," was Fred's comment.

"Hullo, there's that handbill man now," cried Tom, as Giles Frozzler came into the tent. "Won't he laugh when he sees how Sam and Fred have been stuck?"

Two of the circus employees were near by and from their talk Fred learned that the showbill man was the proprietor of the circus.

"He certainly must be a one-horse fellow, or he wouldn't be throwing out his own showbills," said Sam, on hearing this.

Frozzler wore a soft hat, and as he stood near the monkey cage Tom threw some peanuts into the crown of the head covering.

Instantly the monkeys crowded forward. One seized a peanut and another, to get the rest of the nuts, caught hold of the hat and pulled it into the cage.

"Hi! give me my hat!" roared Giles Frozzler, and put his hand into the cage to get the article in question.

The monkeys thought he had more peanuts and, being half starved, they grabbed his hand and pulled it this way and that, while one gave the man a severe nip.

"Oh! oh!" screamed the circus man. "Let go my hand, you pesky rascal!"

"Hullo, dat monkey am got a limb dat don't belong to no tree," sang out Aleck.

"You shut your mouth!" growled Frozzler "Hi! give me my hat!" he went on to the monkeys. But the animals paid no attention to him. They ate up the peanuts as fast as they could and then one began an investigation by pulling the band from the hat.

The head covering was a new one, purchased but two days before, and to see it being destroyed made Giles Frozzler frantic.

"Give me that, you rascals!" he roared, and began to poke at the monkeys with a sharp stick. But two of them caught the stick and, watching their chance, jerked it away from him.

"Hurrah! score one for the monks!" sang out Tom, and this made the crowd laugh.

"If you don't shut up I'll have you put out," came angrily from Giles Frozzler.

38

"Why don't you buy hats for the pool' dear monkeys?" went on Tom. "Then they wouldn't want yours."

"Oh, you keep quiet!"

"Those monkeys are about starved," said Sam. "Let us get up a subscription for their benefit. I don't believe they have had a square meal in a year."

"All of the animals look starved," said Dick, loudly.

"Dat am a fac'," added Aleck.

"This is a bum show," cried a burly farmer boy standing close by. "Why, they have more animals nor this in a dime museum."

"Will you fellows shut up?" cried Giles Frozzler. "This show is all right."

"Of course you'd say so—you're the feller wot put out them bills," said the burly country boy.

"If you don't like the show you can get out."

"All right, Mr. Billman, give me back my quarter."

"Yes, give me my quarter and I'll go too," put in one of the shopkeepers of Oak Run.

"And so will I go," added a woman.

"Me, too," came in a voice from the rear of the crowd.

"Oh, you people make me tired," grumbled Giles Frozzler, and then, fearing that the people would really demand their money back he sneaked off, leaving the monkeys to continue the destruction of his head covering.

CHAPTER XV
ACTS NOT ON THE BILLS

It was now almost time for the ring performance to begin. Dick had purchased so-called reserved seats for the crowd, paying an additional ten cents for each seat, but when they reached the tent with the ring they found that the reserved seats were merely a creation of fancy on the part of the circus owner. Giles Frozzler had had imitation chair bottoms painted on the long boards used for seats and each of these buttons was numbered.

"This is a snide, sure," said Sam.

"Well, there is one thing about it, they can't crowd you," answered Dick. And that was the one advantage the "reserved seats" afforded. On the common seats the spectators were crowded just as closely as possible, until the seats threatened to break down with the weight put upon them.

There was a delay in opening the ring performance and for a very good reason. In the dressing tent Giles Frozzler was having great difficulty in persuading his leading lady rider and his clown to go on. Both wanted their pay for the past two weeks.

"I shall not ride a step until I am paid," said the equestrienne, with a determined toss of her head.

"And I don't do another flip-flap," put in the clown.

"Oh, come, don't talk like that," argued Giles Frozzler. "I'll pay you to-morrow, sure."

"No."

"I'll pay you to-night—just as soon as the performance is over. Just see what a crowd we have—the money is pouring in."

At this the lady bareback rider hesitated, and finally said she would go on. But the clown would not budge.

"I may be a clown in the ring, but not in the dressing room," said he, tartly. "I want my pay, or I don't go on."

"All right then, you can consider yourself discharged," cried Giles Frozzler.

He had started in the circus business as a clown and thought he could very well fill his employee's place for a day or two. In the meantime he would send to the city for another clown whom he knew was out of a situation.

At last the show began with what Frozzler termed on his handbills the Grand Opening Parade, consisting of the two elephants, two ladies on horseback, two circus hands on horseback, the little bear, who was tame, and several educated dogs. In the meantime the band, consisting of seven pieces, struck up a march which was more noise than harmony.

"Here's your grand circus," whispered Sam. "Beats the Greatest Show on Earth to bits, doesn't it?"

"I'll wager a big tomato against a peck of clams that I can get up a better show myself, and do it blindfolded, too," returned Tom.

The grand opening at an end, there was a bit of juggling by a juggler who made several bad breaks in his act, and then came the lady bareback rider. At the same time, Frozzler came out, dressed in a clown's suit and painted up.

"Hullo, there's that chap again!" cried Dick. "He must be running half the show himself."

"How are you to-morrow?" sang out the clown. And after doing a flip-flap, he continued: "Mr. Ringmaster, what's the difference between your knife and me?"

"I know!" shouted Tom. "His knife is a jack-knife, while you are a jack-of-all-trades!"

At this sally there was a loud laugh.

"What is the difference between my knife and you?" queried the ringmaster, as soon as he could make himself heard.

"That's it."

"I don't know."

"I told you!" shouted Tom.

"The difference between your knife and me," answered Frozzler, "is that you can shut your knife up but you can't shut me up," and then he made a face and did another tumble.

"His knife is sharper than you, too," cried Sam. A roar followed, which made Frozzler so angry he shook his fist at the youngest Rover.

"Why is that boy like a fish?" cried Frozzler.

"Because he's too slippery for a clown to catch," put in Fred, loudly, and this created such a laugh that Frozzler's answer was completely lost on the crowd. Again he shook his fist at our friends, but they merely laughed at him.

"I had a funny dream last night," went on the clown. "What do you think I dreamed?"

"That you had paid all your bills," called out Dick.

This brought forth another laugh at Frozzler's expense, in which even some of the circus hands joined.

"Say, those boys are sharp," said the clown who had been discharged. "I shouldn't care to run up against them."

"Three of them are the Rover boys," answered a man sitting near. "Nobody can get the best of them."

"I dreamed a whale came along and swallowed me," went on Frozzler.

"Hullo, I knew you were a Jonah!" sang out Tom. And once more the crowd roared.

"In the whale I met my old schoolmate, Billy Black," continued the clown.

"That was a black moment for poor Billy," was Sam's comment.

"Did you give Billy a whaling?" asked Tom.

"Did dat whale git a stummick ache from swallerin' yo'?" came loudly from Aleck. "I t'ink any whale would, 'less his insides was copper-lined."

Aleck said this so gravely that it brought forth a roar which did not subside for a full minute. Poor Frozzler could do nothing, and to save himself made half a dozen tumbles. Then he started to run from the ring, but tripped over one of the ropes and pitched headlong on his nose.

"Hullo, there a tumble extra!" sang out Tom. "Thank you; nothing like giving us good measure!"

"I'd like to wax that boy good!" growled Giles Frozzler, as he shot into the dressing tent. "Those youngsters spoiled my act completely." And then he hurried to a pail of water to bathe his nose.

The next act was fairly good and put the crowd in good humor once more. But that to follow was so bad that many began to hiss. Then came a race which was as tame as it could possibly be, and many began to leave.

"This is the worst circus yet," said one man. "If anybody comes to-night he'll be sold."

"I'm going to let all my friends know what a flat thing it is," said another. "It isn't worth ten cents, much less a quarter."

The circus was to wind up with the riding of a trick mule,—the animal being brought out by the clown.

As it happened the regular clown and the mule were friends, but the mule hated Frozzler, for the circus owner had on more than one occasion mistreated the animal.

"Be careful of that mule," said one of the hostlers, as he turned the trick animal over to Giles Frozzler. "He's ugly this afternoon."

"Oh, I know how to manage him," growled Frozzler. "Come on here, you imp!" and he hit the mule in the side.

Instantly the mule made a bolt for the ring with Frozzler running after him.

"One hundred dollars to anybody who can ride Hanky-Panky!" sang out Giles Frozzler. "He is as gentle as a kitten, and it is a great pleasure to be able—"

The clown got no further, for just then the mule turned around and gave him a kick which sent him sprawling. Then, like a flash Hanky-Panky turned around, caught Frozzler by the waist and began to run around the ring with him.

"Hi! let go!" screamed the thoroughly frightened circus owner. "Let go, I say! Help! he will kill me! Help!"

"Hurrah! the mule has got the best of it!" sang out Tom. "He knows how to run a circus even if that fellow don't."

"I'll bet on the mule," put in Dick. "He's a nose ahead in this race!"

"Save me!" yelled Frozzler. "Drat that beast! Stop him, somebody!"

There was intense excitement, and several employees rushed forward to rescue Frozzler. But before this could be done, the mule left the ring tent and dashed into the dressing room, where he allowed the circus owner to drop into a barrel of water which was kept there in case of fire. At this the crowd yelled itself hoarse; and this scene brought the afternoon performance to an end.

CHAPTER XVI

ALECK BRINGS NEWS

"I reckon we got square," was Tom's comment, after the fun was over and they were on their way to the farm. "My, but wasn't that circus owner mad!"

"I don't think he'll have another such crowd to-night," said Fred, and he was right. The evening performance was attended by less than a hundred people, and a week later the show failed and was sold out completely.

By the end of the week word was received from both the Stanhopes and the Lanings that all would be glad to join the Rovers in their houseboat vacation. They would take a train for Pittsburg direct on the following Wednesday morning and would there await their friends.

"This suits me to a T!" cried Dick, after reading the communication Dora had sent him. "If we don't have the best time ever then it will be our own fault."

"Just what I say," answered Sam, who had received a long letter from Grace.

There were many articles to pack and ship to Pittsburg. The boys also made out a long list of the things to be purchased for the trip, and in this their father and their aunt helped them.

Sunday passed quietly, all of the boys attending both church and Sunday school. It was a hard matter for Tom to keep still on the Sabbath day, but he did so, much to his aunt's comfort.

Aleck Pop was highly delighted to think that he was to be taken along, especially as cook.

"I'se gwine to do ma level best fo' yo' an' fo' de ladies," said the colored man. "Yo' is gwine to hab reg'lar Waldorf-Astoria feed."

"Don't feed us too good, Aleck, or we'll all die of dyspepsia," said Sam.

"I'll take care of dat, Massah Sam. Don't yo' remember how I used to cook when we was out in de wilderness ob Africa?"

"Indeed I do, Aleck. Yes, I know you'll take care of us," answered Sam.

On the day before the start the boys were surprised to see Hans Mueller appear, with a big trunk and a dress-suit case. The German boy came over from Oak Run in a grocery wagon, having been unable to find a cab.

"How you all vos?" said he, shaking hands. "I dink first I go py dot Pittsburg und den I dinks me I got lost maybe—so I come here."

"That's right, Hans," said Dick. "But what made you bring such a big trunk?"

"Shsh!" answered Hans, putting a finger to the side of his nose. "Dot is a secrets alretty!"

"A secret?"

"Dot's him. You vos going to haf der ladies along, hey?"

"Yes, they are all going."

"I got me dree dress suits py mine drunk in."

"Three dress suits!" roared Dick. "Oh, Hans!"

"Ain't dot enough?" questioned the German cadet, dubiously.

"Three dress suits!" repeated Dick. "Oh, somebody hold me, or I'll have a fit!" And he nearly doubled up with laughter.

"What's the funeral about?" came from Tom, who was standing near.

"Hans is to become a real ladies' man, Tom."

"I don't solve the riddle."

"He has got three dress suits in his trunk."

"Phew! He'll leave us in the shade entirely. Say, Hans, have you got any patent leathers?"

"Yah, I got two pairs of batent-leather shoes."

"Hope you brought your pumps," put in Sam, who had come up.

"Bumps?" queried Hans, with a puzzled look. "Vy I pring me a bump? Does der poat leak?"

"Well, that's the limit!" roared Dick.

"Sam means your dancing pumps?" said Fred. "You mustn't forget them, you know—not if you want to be a really and truly society man."

"I got a pair of slippers for dot," answered Hans. "How many dress suits you vos dake along, hey?"

"Oh, about seven," answered Tom, carelessly.

"You ton't tole me dot, Tom! Maybe I haf to puy some more, hey?"

"Well, I shouldn't—not just yet," answered Dick. "Wait till the new fall styles come out. What you want for a starter is some everyday clothes, a sweater or two, and a pair of rubber boots, in case we have to walk ashore in the mud some time."

"Veil, I got dem too," answered Hans.

A letter had already been sent to Captain Starr, asking him to have the houseboat brought up to Pittsburg. The captain was also told to have the *Dora* thoroughly cleaned and put in proper trim for he outing.

"We want the ladies to be satisfied with her appearance," said Dick.

"And especially since she is named the *Dora*," grinned Tom.

"Oh, you're only piqued because she isn't named the Nellie," retorted his older brother, with a laugh.

"Never mind, Dick; some day you can use the houseboat on a honeymoon," answered Tom, and then ran off.

At last came the time for the boys to leave the farm. Jack Ness took all the trunks and suit cases to the depot and then transported the boys in the family carriage, with Aleck on the seat beside him.

"Good-bye to Valley Brook farm!" cried Tomb waving his hat.

"Take good care of yourselves, boys!" shouted Anderson Rover.

"Don't get drowned," put in the aunt. And then with final adieux they were off. The drive to Oak Run was a quick one, and ten minutes later the train came in and they went aboard.

The run to Pittsburg was to occupy several hours, so the boys made themselves as comfortable as possible. They had dinner on the train and ordered the best of everything to be had.

It had been arranged that all bound for the houseboat trip should meet at the American House, and thither the boys made their way on reaching the Smoky City, as Pittsburg is often called, on account of its numerous manufactories.

"Here we are!" cried a voice, as soon as they entered, and Songbird Powell hurried up to them. "I thought you'd get here about this time."

"Have you seen anything of the ladies?" queried Dick.

"Yes, they are all in the ladies' parlor. I told them I'd keep a lookout for you."

They made their way to the parlor, where a great handshaking took place. Mrs. Stanhope and Dora were there, and also Grace and Nellie with Mrs. Laning. The latter was not used to traveling and was in quite a flutter.

"The girls insisted upon my coming," said Mrs. Laning. "I didn't think I could do it at first, but they wouldn't take no for an answer."

"And we are real glad to have you," answered Dick.

Aleck had been sent off to hunt up Captain Starr and the houseboat, and in the meantime all of the party obtained rooms for the night and then went to supper.

"This puts me in mind of the time we took dinner at Ithaca," said Dick to Dora, on the way to the dining hall. "Do you remember?"

"Indeed I do," she answered, with a pretty blush. "But please do not steer me into the smoking room again," she added, mischievously.

"Don't you think we are going to have a good time, Dora?"

"If I hadn't thought that I shouldn't have come," answered the miss.

It was a happy gathering, and Hans Mueller kept the young folks convulsed by his odd speeches.

"And you ton't vos put no salt py mine coffee in dis dime, Tom," said Hans, referring to a trick which had once been played on him.

"All right, Hansy," answered Tom. "And please don't you pour any coffee down my back," he added, for he had not forgotten how he had been paid back for that joke.

The supper lasted a long time, and after it was over all went to one of the rooms upstairs, where they spent a couple of hours very agreeably.

"We can be thankful that it is such pleasant weather," said Mrs. Stanhope. "An outing on a houseboat during a wet spell would not be so nice."

"Oh, we'd try to make things pleasant," said Tom. "There is a piano on board, and we could have music and singing—"

"A piano! Oh, Tom!" cried Nellie. "How nice! It must be a regular little palace!"

"I haven't seen the boat yet. Uncle Randolph said there was a piano on board."

"And I've got a guitar," came from Songbird Powell.

"With which he will sing to the moon on dark nights," came from Tom.

"I haf got some musics py mine drunk in too," said Hans.

"What have you got, Hansy?" asked Sam—"a tin whistle?"

"No, a music pox vot mine fadder brought from Chermany. He vos a fine pox, too, I can told you."

"That's splendid, Hans," said Dora. "I love a good music box."

So the talk ran on until there was a knock at the door and Aleck appeared. The look on his black face showed that he was excited.

"Say, Massah Dick, I would like to see yo' in private a minute," he said.

"Certainly," replied Dick. "Excuse me," he added, to the others, and went out into the hall with the colored man.

"I didn't want fo' to alarm de ladies," explained Aleck. "But I wanted to tell you as soon as I could."

"Tell me what, Aleck?"

"Dat I dun seen dat rascal, Dan Baxter, less dan half an hour ago," was the answer.

CHAPTER XVII

A QUEER CAPTAIN

"You saw Dan Baxter, here in Pittsburg?" ejaculated Dick.

"Dat's it."

"You are sure you were not mistaken, Aleck? I thought that rascal was miles and miles away."

"Dat's jess wot I dun been thinkin' too. But it was Dan Baxter, suah. I knows him too well to make any mistake about his ugly face."

"Where was he?"

"Dat's de alarmin' part ob it, Massah Dick. Yo' know yo' tole me to find de houseboat."

"Yes."

"Well, I found de boat wid dat dar Cap'n Starr on board, an' we made all dem 'rangements wot you spoke about. Den I started to leave de boat. Dar was an eleckric light on de dock an' a man standing near it, a-watchin' de houseboat. I almost run into him, an' den I discobered it was dat good-fo'-nuffin Dan Baxter."

"He was watching the houseboat?"

"Dat's it."

"Did he recognize you, Aleck?"

"Not till I spoke to him. I said, `Wot yo' doin' heah, Dan Baxter?' When he heard dat he 'most jumped a foot. Den he mutters sumthing wot I couldn't make out an' runs away."

"Did you go after him?"

"Yes, but I couldn't cotch him nohow. Dar was big piles ob boxes an' barrels on de dock and he got away befo' I know wot I was at. I hunted an' hunted, but I couldn't git on his track."

"This is certainly unpleasant, to say the least," mused Dick, biting his lip. "If he is watching us he is doing it for no good purpose."

"Dat's de way. I reasoned. But I didn't want de ladies to heah. Mrs. Stanhope am a powerfully narvous woman."

"Yes, Aleck, you were wise in keeping them in ignorance. But I'll have to tell Tom and Sam and the other fellows, and we'll have to keep our eyes open."

"Is you' goin' to report dis to de police?"

"I may. I'll think it over first. Now, how about the houseboat? Has Captain Starr done as directed?"

"Yes, sah."

"What kind of a man does he seem to he?"

"All right, Massah Dick, only—"

"Only what?" asked the eldest Rover, as he saw the colored servant hesitate.

"Well, to tell de truf, he seems kind of funny to me."

"How funny?"

"Here," and Aleck tapped his forehead.

"Do you mean that he is crazy?"

"Not dat persackly, Massah Dick, but he said sum mighty funny t'ings when we was talkin' acted like he was t'inkin' ob sumt'ing else."

"Humph! Well, if he isn't the sort of fellow we want we'll have to let him go and get another captain."

Dick returned to the apartment he had left and told the others that Aleck had made the necessary arrangements. Then he gave Tom and Sam a wink which meant a good deal. Soon after this the party broke up, and the boys retired to the connecting rooms they had engaged for the night.

"So Aleck saw Dan Baxter!" cried Tom, when told of the news. "That must mean the rascal is on our trail."

"Just what I am thinking, Tom," returned Dick.

"We ought to have the authorities arrest him," put in Sam.

"Perhaps, but we've got to locate him first. Now that he has been discovered he will do his best to keep shady. Maybe he has already left the city."

They talked the matter over for an hour, but could reach no satisfactory conclusion.

"Better take matters as they come," said Powell. "He won't dare to molest you openly."

"No, but he will molest us in secret, which will be worse," replied Sam.

"None of the ladies or the girls must hear of this," said Tom. "It would spoil their whole trip, even if Baxter didn't show himself again."

"I ton't oben mine mouds apout noddings," declared Hans. "I vos so quiet like an ellerfaunt in a church!"

Bright and early the boys were astir on the following morning, and Dick, Tom, and Sam went off to interview Captain Starr before breakfast. They found the captain a thick-set fellow, with a heavy mustache and big, bushy whiskers. He had eyes of the dreamy sort, which generally looked away when speaking to anybody.

"This is Captain Starr?" said Dick, addressing him.

"I'm your man."

"I am Dick Rover, and these are my brothers, Tom and Sam."

Dick put out his hand, but the captain merely nodded.

"Is everything ready for the trip, captain?" asked Tom.

"Yes, sir."

"You had the boat cleaned up?" said Sam.

"Yes, sir."

"We'll look her over," said Dick.

"Yes, sir."

They walked over the houseboat from end to end. The craft was certainly a beauty and as clean as a whistle. There was a living room, a dining room, a kitchen, and eight sleeping rooms—four of the latter downstairs and four upstairs. Each sleeping room contained two berths. There was also a bunk room below, for the help, and a small room for the captain. In the living room, was the piano and also a bookcase containing half a hundred choice novels.

"This is certainly great," said Tom.

"Better than I thought it would be," answered Sam. "It's a perfect palace."

"And see how the brasswork shines," went on Tom. "The captain certainly had things cleaned up.

45

"But he is a queer stick, if ever there was one." came from Dick, in a whisper. "I must say, I don't half like him."

"He acts as if he was asleep," was Tom's comment.

"Or else as if he had something on his mind."

"Anyway, he comes highly recommended," said Sam.

When they came out on the deck they found Captain Starr sitting on a bench smoking a corncob pipe.

"She is in fine shape and I congratulate you, captain," said Dick, pleasantly.

"Thank you," was the short answer.

"You will be ready to have us taken down the river as soon as we get our things on board?"

"Yes, sir."

"Confound him," thought Dick. "Why doesn't he say something else? He is a regular automaton."

"By the way, captain," put in Tom, "have you noticed a stranger watching the *Dora* the last night or two?"

At this question Captain Starr leaped to his feet, allowing his corncob pipe to fall to the ground.

"What made you ask that question?" he demanded.

"We have an enemy, named Dan Baxter. We suspect he is following us and is spying on us."

"Yes, I have seen a young fellow around half a dozen times. In fact, I caught him on the houseboat once."

"You did!" cried Dick. "What was he doing?"

"Going through the stuff in the living room."

"What did you do to him?"

"I yelled at him, demanding to know what he wanted. As soon as he heard me he ran ashore and disappeared."

"Did you try to find him?"

"No, because I didn't want to leave the houseboat alone."

"Did you see him last night—while our colored man was here?"

"I saw somebody, but it was too dark to make out exactly who it was."

CHAPTER XVIII
ON BOARD THE HOUSEBOAT

After questioning Captain Starr as closely as possible all three of the Rover boys came to the conclusion that it must have been Dan Baxter who had visited the *Dora* on the sly.

"I don't like this at all," said Sam. "He is going to make trouble for us—no two ways about that."

"The best thing to do, in my opinion, is to get away without delay," said Tom. "He won't find it so easy to follow us then."

"I'm going to throw him off the scent," said Dick.

"How?"

"By pretending to go to one place, while we can really go to another."

"That's a scheme."

A small tug had been chartered to tow the houseboat, and the captain of this was ordered to be ready for moving at eleven o'clock.

"We shall go to Camdale first," said Dick, naming a place about forty miles away.

"All right, sir—wherever you say," said the tug commander.

Returning to the hotel, the boys found the others finishing breakfast and sat down to their own. They said the *Dora* was in perfect trim and that the trip down the Ohio was to begin without delay.

"Well, I am sure I am ready," said Nellie. "I am just dying to see the houseboat."

Aleck hurried around to buy the necessary stores, which were taken to the *Dora* in a wagon, Then two carriages brought down the ladies and the boys and a truck brought along the baggage.

"What a beautiful boat!" cried Dora after going on board. "And how tidy everything is!"

"Then you are not ashamed to have her called the *Dora?*" said Dick, well satisfied.

"Ashamed? Oh, Dick, I am delighted!"

"This boat is a gem," was Songbird Powell's comment. "Say, folks on the Ohio will take us, to be millionaires."

"Dis ship is besser dan a ferrypoat," was Hans' comment.

"A ferryboat!" shrieked Grace. "Oh, Hans!"

"I mean von of dem double-decker ferrypoats vot runs from New York to Chersey City—dem kind vot has got blate-glass vinders und looking-glasses der sthairs on," explained the German cadet. "Da vos peauties, too."

"If we don't enjoy this trip it will be our fault," said Fred.

The lines were cast off, the steam tug puffed, and in a moment more the houseboat had left the dock and the voyage down the Ohio was begun.

"I'll not be sorry to leave Pittsburg behind," said Nellie. "There is so much smoke."

"Well, they have to have smoke—in such a hive of industry," answered Dick.

By noon Pittsburg and Allegheny were left behind and once more the sky was clear and blue above them. The sun shone brightly and there was just enough breeze to keep the air cool and delicious. All sat on the forward deck, under a wide-spread awning, watching the scenery as they floated onward.

After a consultation it was decided that the first stop should be made at a small village on the river called Pleasant Hills. Mrs. Laning had a friend there whom she had not seen for years, and she said she would be pleased to make a call.

"All right," said Dick, "Pleasant Hills it is." And he called to the tug captain and gave the necessary directions.

"That will throw Dan Baxter off the track a little," whispered Sam.

Aleck Pop was highly pleased with the cooking arrangements. There was a first-class gasolene stove, and the kitchen was fitted with all sorts of appliances for rendering cooking easy.

"I'se gwine to do my best fo' you," said the colored man, and dinner, which was served at one o'clock, proved to be little short of a genuine feast, with oxtail soup, breast of lamb, mashed potatoes, green peas, lettuce, coffee, pudding and cheese.

"Why, Aleck, this is a surprise," said Dora. "Some day they will want you to become the chef in a big hotel." And this compliment tickled the colored man greatly.

"T'ank yo' Miss Dora," he answered. "But I don't want to be no chef in a hotel. All I wants to do is to stay wid de Rober boys so long as I lib."

During the afternoon the boys tried their hands at fishing and caught quite a mess. By four o'clock Pleasant Hills was reached and they tied up in a convenient spot. All of the girls and Mrs. Stanhope went ashore with Mrs. Laning, to visit the friend that had been mentioned.

"Bring them down to the houseboat to-night, if they care to come," said Dick.

"Thank you, Dick, perhaps we will," answered Mrs. Laning.

"Let us take a swim while they are gone," suggested Tom. "That water is too inviting to resist."

"Agreed!" shouted the others, and ran to their rooms, to get out their bathing suits. Soon Tom was ready, and leaping to the end of the houseboat, took a straight dive into the river. Sam followed and Fred came next, and then Dick, Songbird, and Hans came down in a bunch. The water was just cold enough to be pleasant, and they splashed around in great sport.

"This is what I call living!" yelled Tom and diving under, he caught Hans by the big toe.

"Hi, hi! let go mine does!" shrieked the German lad. "Somedings has me py der does cotched!"

"Maybe it's a shark," suggested Fred.

"A shark! Vos der sharks py der Ohio River?"

"Tons of them," came from Sam. "Look out, Hansy, or they'll swallow you."

"Du meine Zeit!" gasped the German cadet. "Vy didn't you tole me dot pefore, hey? I guess I don't schwim no more." And he started to climb up a rope ladder leading to the deck of the houseboat.

"Don't go, Hans!" sang out Songbird. "They are fooling you."

"Dere ton't been no sharks in der river?"

"No, nothing but sawfish and whales."

"A vale! Dot's chust so bad like a shark."

"No, not at all. A shark bites. A whale simply swallows you alive," put in Sam, with a grin.

"Swallows me alife, hey? Not on your life he ton't!" returned Hans, and started again for the rope ladder. But Sam pulled him back and ducked him, and was in turn ducked by Fred, who went under by a shove from Dick; and then followed a regular mix-up, the water flying in all directions.

"By golly, dat's great!" cried Aleck, from the deck. "I dun' t'ink a lot ob eels was dancin' a jig down dar!"

"Come down here, Aleck, and get some of the black washed off!" shouted Tom, gleefully.

"Not fo' a dollah, Massah Tom—leasewise, not while yo' is around."

"What are you afraid of?" asked Tom, innocently.

"Yo' is too full ob tricks fo' dis chile. When I wants a baf I'se gwine to take dat baf in a tub, an' when yo' ain't around," answered Aleck. "Yo' am—Oh—wough!" And then the colored man retreated in great haste, for Tom had sent up a shower of water all over him.

"Here comes a big river boat!" cried Songbird, presently. "Let us go out and catch the rollers!" And out they swam and waited until the swells, several feet high, came rolling in. It was immense fun bobbing up and down like so many corks.

"Wish the steamers would continue to come past," said Fred. "This suits me to death."

"Here comes another pretty big boat," answered Tom. "And she is closer to shore than that other craft, so we'll get the rollers at their best."

"Don't get too close," cried Songbird. "I knew a fellow who did that once and got sucked under."

On came the river boat and was soon opposite to where the houseboat lay. She carried only a few passengers, but a very large quantity of freight.

"Here she comes!" cried Fred. "Now for some more fun."

"Don't get too close!" repeated Songbird, but Tom did not heed him and went within fifty feet of the steamboat's side. The rollers here were certainly large, but all of a sudden Tom appeared to lose interest in the sport.

"Hullo, Tom! What are you so quiet about?" sang out Dick in alarm.

"Perhaps he has a cramp," put in Sam. "Tom, are you all right?" he cried.

"Yes, I'm all right," was the answer, and then Tom swam to his brothers with all speed. The steamboat was now well on its way down the Ohio.

"What is it?" asked Dick, feeling that something was wrong. "If you have had even a touch of a cramp you had better get out, Tom."

"I haven't any cramp. Did you see them?"

"Them? Who?"

"The two fellows at the stern of that boat?"

"No. What of them?"

"One was Dan Baxter and the other was Lew Flapp."

CHAPTER XIX

WORDS AND BLOWS

"Baxter and Flapp!"

The cry came from several at once, and all climbed to the deck of the houseboat after Tom.

"Are you certain of this, Tom?" asked Dick.

"Yes, I saw them as plain as day. They were looking at the houseboat."

"Did they see you?"

"I think they did, and if so they must have seen the rest of our crowd too."

"We ought to go after them," came from Fred. "The name of that steamboat was the *Beaver*."

"Wonder where she will make her first stop?"

For an answer to this question Captain Starr was appealed to, and he said the craft would most likely stop first at a town which we will call Penwick.

"How far is that from here?" asked Sam.

"About six miles."

"Can we get a train to that place?"

"Yes, but I don't know when."

A time-table was consulted, and it was found that no train could be had from Pleasant Hills to Penwick for two hours and three-quarters.

"That is too late for us," said Dick. "If they saw Tom they'll skip the moment the steamboat touches the landing."

"If you want to catch them why don't you follow them up in the tug?" suggested Songbird.

"Dot's the talk!" came from Hans. "I would like to see you cotch dot Flapp and Paxter mineselluf."

"I'll use the tug," said Dick.

He summoned the captain and explained the situation. It was found that steam on the tug was low, but Captain Carson said he would get ready to move down the stream with all possible speed.

"I would like you to stay on the houseboat," said Dick, to Songbird, Fred, and Hans. "I don't want to leave Captain Starr in charge all alone."

So it was agreed; and fifteen minutes later the tug was on the way after the *Beaver*, with Dick, Tom, and Sam on board.

"Can we catch the steamboat, captain?" questioned Tom, anxiously.

"We can try," was the answer. "If I had known you wanted to use the tug again to-night I should have kept steam up."

"Well, we didn't know."

The *Beaver* was out of sight and they did not see the steamboat again until she was turning in at the Penwick dock.

"There she is!" cried Sam.

"Hurry up, Captain Carson!" called out Dick. "If you don't hurry we will lose the fellows we are after, sure."

"I am hurrying as much as I can," replied the captain.

In five minutes more they gained one end of the dock and the Rovers leaped ashore. The *Beaver* was at the other end, discharging passengers at one gang plank and freight at another.

"See anything of them?" asked Sam.

"Yes, there they are!" shouted Tom, and pointed to the street beyond the dock.

"I see them," returned Dick. "Come on!" And he started for the street, as swiftly as his feet could carry him.

He was well in advance of Sam and Tom when Dan Baxter, looking back, espied him.

"Hi, Flapp, we must leg it!" cried Baxter, in quick alarm.

"Eh?" queried Lew Flapp. "What's wrong now?"

"They are after us!"

"Who?"

"The three Rover Boys. Come on!"

The former bully of Putnam Hall glanced back and saw that Dan Baxter (and he too had been a bully at the Hall) was right.

"Where shall we go to?" he asked in sudden fright.

"Follow me!" And away went Dan Baxter up the street with Flapp at his heels. Dick, Tom, and Sam came after them, with a number of strangers between.

"Do you think we can catch them?" asked Tom.

"We've got to catch them," answered Dick. "If you see a policeman tell him to come along—that we are after a couple of criminals."

Having passed up one street for a block, Baxter and Flapp made a turn and pursued their course down a thoroughfare running parallel to the river.

Here were located a number of factories and mills, with several tenement houses and low groggeries between.

"They are after us yet," panted Flapp, after running for several minutes. "Say, I can't keep this up much longer."

"Come in here," was Dan Baxter's quick reply, and he shot into a small lumber yard attached to a box factory. It was now after six o'clock and the factory had shut down for the day.

Once in the lumber yard they hurried around several corners, and presently came to a shed used for drying lumber. From this shed there was a small door leading into the factory proper.

"I reckon we are safe enough here," said Dan Baxter, as they halted in the shed and crouched down back of a pile of boards.

"Yes, but we can't stay here forever," replied Lew Flapp.

"We can stay as long as they hang around, Flapp."

In the meantime the Rover Boys reached the entrance to the yard, and Dick, who had kept the lead, called a halt.

"I am pretty certain they ran in here," he declared.

"Then let us root them out," said Tom. "And the quicker the better."

The others were willing, and they entered the small lumber yard without hesitation. As there were but three wagonways, each took one, and all presently reached the entrance to the drying shed.

"See anybody?" questioned Dick.

"No," came from his brothers.

"Neither did I. I see there is a big brick wall around this yard. If they came in here they must have gone into this shed or into the factory itself."

"That's it, Dick," said Tom. He pushed open the door to the shed. "I'm going to investigate."

"So am I," said both of the others.

In the shed all was dark and soon Sam stumbled over some blocks of wood and fell headlong.

"Confound the darkness," he muttered. "We ought to have brought a light."

"I've got one," answered Dick, and feeling in his pocket he produced one of the new-style electric pocket lights. He pushed the button and instantly the light flashed out, as from a bull's-eye lantern.

"Hurrah, that's a good thing!" cried Tom. "By the way, isn't it queer there is no watchman here?"

"Maybe the night watchman hasn't got around yet," answered Dick, and struck the truth.

They began to move around the shed, much to the alarm of both Dan Baxter and Lew Flapp.

"I don't see any trace—" began Dick, when of a sudden the light landed fairly and squarely on Baxter's face. Then it shifted to the face of Lew Flapp.

"The old Harry take you, Dick Rover!" yelled Baxter, in a sudden rage, and throwing his whole weight against the pile of boards on which the eldest Rover was standing, he caused it to go over, hurling Dick flat on his back on the floor.

"Dick, are you hurt?" called out Tom. The electric light had been broken, and all was pitch-dark.

"I—I guess—not," answered Dick. "But it was a close shave."

"They are getting out!" came from Sam, as he heard a scuffling of feet.

"No—they are going into the factory," shouted Tom. "Stop, Baxter! Stop, Flapp! If you don't—Oh!"

Tom's cry came to a sudden end, for without warning a billet of wood struck him fairly on top of the head and he went down as if shot.

By this time Dick was on his feet.

"What's up, Tom?"

"I—I—oh, my head?"

"Did somebody hit you?"

"Yes."

Sam was running after Baxter and Flapp. But they reached the factory first and banged the door full in the face of the youngest Rover.

"Open that door, Dan Baxter!" called out Sam.

"All right!" was the sudden reply, and open flew the door. Then down on poor Sam's head came a heavy billet of wood and he pitched backward unconscious. Then the door was closed once more and locked from the inside.

CHAPTER XX
DAYS OF PLEASURE

"Sam! Sam! Speak to us!"

It was Dick who uttered the words, as he knelt beside his youngest brother and caught his hands. Tom was just staggering up.

But Sam was past speaking, and made no reply.

"What's the matter, Dick?" asked Tom.

"Poor Sam is knocked out completely. I don't know but what they have killed him."

"Oh, don't say that!"

"Have you got a match? I've lost that electric pocket light."

"Yes." Tom struck the match and lit a bit of pine wood that was handy, and found the light. "Dick, don't tell me he is dead."

"Oh!" came in a deep gasp from poor Sam, and he gave a shiver from head to feet.

"He isn't dead, but they must have hit him a terrible blow. Let us carry him out into the open air."

This they did, and laid the youngest Rover on some boards. Here he presently opened his eyes and stared about him.

"Don't—don't hit me again!" he pleaded, vacantly.

"They shan't hit you again, Sam," answered Dick, tenderly. He felt of his brother's head. On top was a lump, from which the blood was flowing.

"This is the worst yet," said Tom. "What had we best do next?"

"Call a policeman, if you can find any."

"That's rather a hard thing to do around here."

51

However, Tom ran off, and while he was gone Dick did what little he could to make Sam comfortable. At last the youngest Rover opened his eyes again and struggled to sit up.

"Where—where are they, Dick?"

"Gone into the factory."

"Oh, my head!"

"It was a wicked blow, Sam. But keep still if your head hurts."

When Tom came back he was accompanied by a watchman from a neighboring yard and presently they were joined by the watchman of the box factory, who had been to a corner groggery, getting a drink.

"What's the row?" questioned the first watchman, and when told, emitted a low whistle.

"I think those fellows are in the factory yet," continued Dick.

As soon as the second watchman came up both went into the box factory and were gone fully ten minutes. Then Dick followed them, since Sam was rapidly recovering.

"Can't find them," said one of the watchmen. "But yonder window is open. They must have dropped into that yard and run away."

"Is the window generally closed?"

"Yes."

"Then you must be right."

"Why don't you call up the police? You can do it on the telephone."

"Have you a telephone here?"

"Of course."

Dick went to the telephone and told the officer in charge at the station what had occurred.

"I'll send two men at once," said the officer over the wire; and in five minutes the policemen appeared.

Again there was a search, not only of the box factory, but also of the whole neighborhood, but no trace of Dan Baxter or Lew Flapp could be found.

Having bathed their hurts, both Sam and Tom felt better, and all three of the Rovers walked to the police station with the policemen, and there told the full particulars of their story.

"You were certainly in hard luck," said the police captain, who happened to be in charge. "I'll do what I can to round these rascals up." But nothing came of this, for both Baxter and Flapp left Penwick that very night.

When the Rover boys returned to the houseboat, it was long after midnight, but none on board had gone to bed. The Stanhopes and Lanings had come back, bringing their friends with them, and all had been surprised to find the Rovers absent. After remaining on the houseboat a couple of hours the friends had gone home again.

"Something is wrong; I can see it in your looks, Dick," said Dora, as she came to him.

"Sam, where did you get that hurt on your head?" questioned Grace, in alarm.

"Oh, we had a little trouble, but it didn't amount to much," answered the youngest Rover as bravely as he could.

"Yes, but your head is in a dreadful condition."

"And Tom has a cut over the left eye," burst in Nellie. "Oh, you have had a fight of some kind, and I know it!"

"A fight!" cried Mrs. Stanhope. "Is it possible that you have been fighting?"

"We had a brush with a couple of rascals in Penwick," said Dick. "We tried to catch them, but they got away from us. That is all there is to it. I'd rather not talk about it," he went on, seeing that Mrs. Laning also wanted to ask questions.

"Well, you must really be more careful in the future," said Mrs. Stanhope. "I suppose they wanted to rob you."

"They didn't get the chance to rob us," put in Tom, and then the Rovers managed to change the subject. The Stanhopes and the Lanings did not dream that Dan Baxter and Lew Flapp had caused the trouble. Perhaps, in the light of later events, it would have been better had they been told the truth.

Dick gave orders that the *Dora* should be moved down the river early the next day, and before the majority of the party were up, Pleasant Hills was left behind.

"I sincerely trust we have seen the last of Baxter and Flapp," said Sam.

"So do I, Sam," answered Dick.

"I'd like to meet them and punch their heads good for them," came from Tom.

After that a week slipped by with very little out of the ordinary happening. Day after day the houseboat moved down the river, stopping at one place or another, according to the desires of those on board. The weather continued fine, and the boys and girls enjoyed themselves immensely in a hundred different ways. All had brought along bathing suits and took a dip every day. They also fished, and tramped through the woods at certain points along the stream. One night they went ashore in a field and camped out, with a big roaring fire to keep them company.

"This is the way it was when the cadets went into camp," said Dick. "I can tell you, we had lots of sport."

"It must have been very nice, Dick," answered Dora. "Sometimes I wish I was a boy and could go to Putnam Hall."

"Not much! I'd rather have you a girl!" declared Dick, and in the dark he gave her hand a tight squeeze.

During those days Dick noticed that Captain Starr acted more peculiar than ever. At times he would talk pleasantly enough, but generally he was so close-mouthed that one could scarcely get a word out of him.

"I believe he is just a wee bit off in his upper story," said the oldest Rover. "But I don't imagine it is enough to count."

"If he had any ambition in him he wouldn't be satisfied to run a houseboat," said Tom. "It's about the laziest job I know of."

The Monday after this talk found the *Dora* down the Ohio as far as Louisville. To avoid the falls in the stream, the houseboat had been taken through the canal, and during the middle of the afternoon was taken down the stream a distance of perhaps eighteen miles, to Skemport,—so named after Samuel Skem, a dealer in Kentucky thoroughbreds.

Fred Garrison had a friend who came from Skemport and wanted to visit him. The others were willing, and Fred went off with Tom and Sam as soon as the boat was tied up. When they came back, late in the evening, the others were told that the friend had invited all hands to visit a large stock farm in that vicinity the next afternoon to look at the horses there.

"That will be nice!" cried Dora. "I love a good horse."

Two large carriages were hired for the purpose, and Aleck was allowed to drive one, a man from the local livery stable driving the other.

"How soon will you be back?" sang out Captain Starr after them.

"Can't say exactly," replied Dick.

The distance to the stock farm was three miles, but it was quickly covered, and once there the Rovers and their friends were made to feel perfectly at home.

"I'd like to go horseback riding on one of those horses," said Dora, after inspecting a number of truly beautiful steeds.

"You shall," said the owner of the stock farm; and a little later Dora, Nellie, Dick, and Tom were in the saddle and off for a gallop of several miles, never once speculating on how that ride was to end.

CHAPTER XXI
THE DISAPPEARANCE OF THE HOUSEBOAT

Never was a girl more light-hearted than was Dora when in the saddle on the Kentucky thoroughbred. And her cousin was scarcely less elated.

"Let us have a little race, Nellie," cried Dora. "It will be lots of fun."

"Oh, we don't want the horses to run away," answered Nellie.

"I don't think they will run away."

The race was started, and to give the girls a chance, Dick and Tom dropped to the rear. Soon a turn of the road hid the two girls from view.

"Wait a minute—there is something wrong with my saddle," said Tom, a moment later, and he came to a halt and slipped to the ground.

Dick would have preferred going on, but did not wish to leave his brother alone, so he also halted. A buckle had broken and it took some time to repair the damage, so Tom could continue his ride.

"The girls have disappeared," said Dick, on making the turn ahead in the road.

They came to a spot where the road divided into three forks and halted in perplexity.

"Well, this is a nuisance," declared Tom, after scratching his head. "I suppose they thought we were watching them."

"More than likely."

"Which road shall we take?"

"Bless me if I know."

"Well, we can't take all three."

They stared at the hoofprints in the road, but there were too many of them to make anything of the marks.

"Stumped!" remarked Tom, laconically.

"Let us wait a while. Perhaps, when the girls see we are not following, they will turn back."

"All right; but we've made a fine pair of escorts, haven't we, Dick?"

"We are not responsible for that buckle breaking."

"That's so, too."

They waited for several minutes, but the girls did not appear.

"Supposing I take to one road and you to the other?" said Dick. "If you see them, whistle."

"What about the third road?" And Tom grinned.

"We'll leave that for the present."

Off they set, and as ill-luck would have it took the two roads the girls had not traveled. Each went fully a mile before he thought of coming back.

"Well, what luck?" asked Dick, as he rode up.

"Nothing doing, Dick."

"Ditto."

"Then they must have taken to the third road."

"That's it,—unless they rode faster than we did."

"Shall I try that other road?"

"You can if you wish. I'll stay here. If they come back, we can wait for you," added the oldest Rover.

Once more Tom set off. But he had pushed his horse so fast before the animal was now tired and had to take his time in traveling.

The third road led down to the river front, and before a great while the water's edge was reached. Here there were numerous bushes and trees and the road turned and ran some distance along the bank.

"Well, I'm stumped and no mistake," murmured the fun-loving Rover, "I felt sure—"

He broke off short, for a distance scream had reached his ears.

"Was that Nellie's voice?" he asked himself, and then strained his ears, for two more screams had reached him. "Nellie, and Dora too, as sure as fate!" he ejaculated. "Something has happened to them! Perhaps those horses are running away!"

He hardly knew how to turn, for the trees and bushes cut off his view upon every side. He galloped along the road, which followed the windings of the Ohio. But try his best he could locate neither girls nor horses.

It was maddening, and the cold sweat stood out upon Tom's forehead. Something was very much wrong, but what was it?

"Nellie! Dora! Where are you?" he called out. "*Where are you?*"

Only the faint breeze in the trees answered him.

"I've got to find them!" he groaned. "I've got to! That is all there is to it." He repeated the words over and over again. "What will Mrs. Laning and Mrs. Stanhope say, and Grace?"

Again he went on, but this time slower than before, looking to the right and the left and ahead. Not a soul was in sight. The road was so cut up he could make nothing of the hoofmarks which presented themselves.

"This is enough to drive one insane," he reasoned. "Where in the world did they go to? I'd give a thousand dollars to know."

At last he reached a point where the road ran close to the water's edge. He looked out on the river. Only a distant steamboat and a small sailboat were in view.

"Wonder if they rode down to where we left the houseboat?" he asked himself. "She must be somewhere in this vicinity. Maybe they have only been fooling us."

Although Tom told himself this, there was no comfort in the surmise. He moved on once more. It was now growing dark and there were signs of a coming storm in the air.

At last he reached a spot which looked somewhat familiar to him. He came down to the water's edge once more.

"Why—er—I thought the houseboat was here," he said, half aloud. "This looks like the very spot."

But no houseboat was there, and scratching his head once more, Tom concluded that he had made a mistake.

"I'm upset if ever a fellow was," he thought. "Well, no wonder. Such happenings as these are enough to upset anybody."

Tom knew of nothing more to do than to return to where he had left Dick, and this he did as quickly as the tired horse would carry him.

"No success, eh?" said the oldest Rover. "What do you make of it, Tom?"

When he had heard his brother's tale he grew unusually grave.

"You are sure you heard them scream?" he questioned, anxiously.

"I'm sure of nothing—now. I thought I was sure about the houseboat, but I wasn't," answered Tom, bluntly. "I'm all mixed up."

"I'll go down there with you," was the only answer Dick made.

It did not take long to reach the spot. It was now dark and a mist was rising from the river.

"This is certainly the spot where we tied up," declared the oldest Rover. "Why, I helped to drive that stake myself."

"Then the houseboat is gone!"

"That's the size of it."

"And the girls are gone too," went on Tom. "Yes, but the two happenings may have no connection, Tom."

"Don't be so sure of that!"

"What do you mean?"

"I'm thinking about Dan Baxter and Lew Flapp. They wouldn't be above stealing the houseboat."

"I believe you there."

"And if those girls happened to go on board—Look there!"

Tom pointed out in the darkness on the road. Two horses were coming toward them, each wearing a lady's saddle and each riderless.

"There are the horses," said Dick. "But the girls? You think—"

"The girls came down here on their horses and dismounted, to go on board of the houseboat."

"Well, where is the houseboat?"

It was a question neither of them could answer. They looked out on the river, but the mist hung over everything like a pall.

"Dick, I am afraid something serious has happened," came from Tom, ominously. "Those screams weren't uttered for nothing."

"Let us make a closer examination of the shore," answered the oldest Rover, and they did so. They found several hoofprints of horses, but that was all.

"I can't see any signs of a struggle," said Tom.

"Nor I. And yet, if those rascals ran off with the houseboat and with the girls on board, how would they square matters with Captain Starr?"

"And with Captain Carson? The tug is gone, too."

"Yes, but the tug went away when we did, and wasn't to come back until to-morrow morning. Captain Carson said he would have to coal up, over to one of the coal docks."

"Then some other tug must have towed the houseboat away."

"Either that or they are letting the *Dora* drift with the current."

"That would be rather dangerous around here,—and in the mist. A steamer might run the houseboat down."

The brothers knew not what to do. To go back to the stock farm with the news that both the girls and the houseboat were missing was extremely distasteful to them.

"This news will almost kill Mrs. Stanhope," said Dick.

"Well, it will be just as bad for Mrs. Laning, Dick."

"Not exactly,—she has Grace left, while Dora. is Mrs. Stanhope's only child."

Once again the two boys rode up and down the' Ohio for a distance of nearly a mile. At none of the docks or farms could they catch the least sign of the houseboat.

"She may be miles from here by this time," said Dick, with almost a groan. "There is no help for it, Tom, we've got to go back and break the news as best we can."

"Very well," answered Tom, soberly. Every bit of fun was knocked out of him, and his face was as long as if he was going to a funeral.

Dick felt equally bad. Never until that moment had he realized how dear Dora Stanhope was to him. He would have given all he possessed to be able to go to her assistance.

The mist kept growing thicker, and by the time the stock farm was reached it was raining in torrents. But the boys did not mind this discomfort as they rode along, leading the two riderless saddle horses. They had other things more weighty to think about.

CHAPTER XXII
DAN BAXTER'S LITTLE GAME

In order to ascertain just what did become of the houseboat, it will be necessary to go back to the time when the *Dora* was tied up near the village of Skemport.

Not far away from Skemport was a resort called the Stock Breeders' Rest—a cross-roads hotel where a great deal of both drinking and gambling was carried on.

During the past year Dan Baxter had become passionately fond of card playing for money and he induced Lew Flapp to accompany him to the Stock Breeders' Rest.

"We can have a fine time there," said Baxter. "And as the Rovers' houseboat will not be far off, we can keep our eyes on that crowd and watch our chance to deal them another blow."

Lew Flapp was now reckless and ready for almost anything, and he consented. They hired a room at the cross-roads hotel, and that night both went to the smoking room to look at what was going on.

A professional gambler from Kentucky soon discovered them, and he induced Dan Baxter to lay with him,—after learning that Lew Flapp had no money to place on a game. Baxter and the gambler played that night and also the next morning, and as a result Baxter lost about every dollar he had with him.

"You cheated me," he cried passionately, when his last dollar was gone. "You cheated me, and I'll have the police arrest you!"

This accusation brought on a bitter quarrel, and fearful that they might be killed by the gambler and his many friends who frequented the resort, Dan Baxter and Lew Flapp fled for their lives. They were followed by two thugs, and to escape molestation took refuge in a stable on the outskirts of Skemport and only a short distance from where the *Dora* lay.

"How much money did you lose, Baxter?" asked Flapp, after they had made certain that they were safe for the time being.

"Two hundred and sixty-five dollars—every dollar I had with me," was the gloomy response.

"Is it possible!" gasped Lew Flapp. He wondered what they were going to do without money.

"What have you got left of the money I loaned you?" went on Baxter.

"Just two dollars and twenty cents."

"Humph! That's a long way from being a fortune," grumbled the discomfited leader of the evil-doers.

"You are right. I think you were foolish to gamble."

"Oh, don't preach!"

"I'm not preaching. What shall we do next?"

"I don't know. If I was near some big city I might draw some money from a bank."

"You might go to Louisville."

"No, I'd be sure to have trouble if I went to that place—I had trouble there before."

They looked around them, and were surprised to see the houseboat in plain view. This interested them, and they watched the *Dora* with curiosity.

"If we had a houseboat we could travel in fine style," was Lew Flapp's comment.

"Just the thing, Flapp!" cried Dan Baxter.

"Perhaps; but you can't buy a houseboat for two dollars and twenty cents, nor charter one either."

"We won't buy one or charter one," was Dan Baxter's crafty answer.

"Eh?"

"We'll borrow that one. She's a fairy and will just suit us, Flapp."

"I don't quite understand. You're not fool enough to think the Rovers will let you have their houseboat."

"Of course not. But if I take possession while they are away—"

"How do you know they will be away—I mean all of them at one time?"

"I'll fix it so they are. We must watch our chance. I can send them a decoy message, or something like that."

"You'll have to be pretty shrewd to get the best of the Rovers."

"Pooh! They are not so wise as you think. They put on a big front, but that is all there is to it," went on Dan Baxter, loftily.

"Well, go ahead; I don't care what you do."

"You'll help me; won't you?"

"Certainly,—if the risk isn't too great. We don't want to get caught and tried for stealing."

"Leave it all to me, Flapp."

As we know, fortune for once favored Dan Baxter. From the stable he and Flapp saw the party depart for the stock farm, leaving nobody but Captain Starr in charge. They also saw the steam tug move away, to get a new supply of coal in her bunkers.

"Everything is coming our way," chuckled Dan Baxter, with a wicked grin on his scarred face. "Flapp, the coast is almost clear."

"Almost, but not quite. That captain is still on board."

"Oh, that chap is a dough-head. We can easily make him do what we want."

"Don't be too sure. He might watch 'his chance and knock us both overboard."

"Well, I know how to fix him. I'll send him a message to come here—that Dick Rover wants him. When he comes we can bind him fast with this old harness and leave him here."

"And after that, what?"

"We'll drop down the river a way. Then we can paint a new name on the boat, get a steam tug, and make off for the Mississippi,—and the Rovers and their friends can go to grass."

This programme looked inviting to Flapp, and when Dan Baxter wrote a note to the captain of the *Dora* he volunteered to deliver it. He found Captain Starr on the front deck of the houseboat smoking his corncob as usual.

The captain had one of his peculiar moods on him, and it took a minute or two for Flapp to make him understand about the note. But he fell into the trap with ease and readily consented to follow the young rascal to the stable.

As he entered the open doorway, Dan Baxter came at him from behind, hitting him in the head with a stout stick. The captain went down half stunned.

"See—see here," he gasped. "Wha—what does this—"

"Shut up!" cried Baxter. "We won't hurt you if you'll keep still. But if you don't—"

"I—I haven't hurt anybody, sir."

"All right, old man; keep still."

"But I—I don't understand?"

"You will, later on."

Dan Baxter had the straps of the old harness ready and with them he fastened Captain Starr's hands behind him and also tied his ankles together. Then he backed the commander of the houseboat to a post and secured him, hands and feet.

"Now then, don't you make any noise until to-morrow morning," was Dan Baxter's warning. "If you do, you'll get into trouble. If you keep quiet, we'll come back in the morning, release you, and give you a hundred dollars."

"Give me a hundred dollars?" questioned the captain, simply.

"That is what I said."

"Then I had better keep quiet. But the houseboat—"

"The houseboat will be left just where it is."

"Oh, all right, sir," and the captain breathed a sigh of relief. That he was just a little simple-minded was beyond question.

Leaving the captain a prisoner, Dan Baxter and Lew Flapp made their way with caution toward the houseboat. As they had surmised, the *Dora* was now totally deserted. They leaped on the deck and entered the sumptuous living room.

"This is fine," murmured Lew Flapp. "They must be living like nabobs on this craft."

"You're right. A piano and a guitar, too." Baxter passed into the dining room. "Real silver on the table. Flapp, we've struck luck."

"Sure."

"That silver is worth just so much money,—when we need the funds."

"Would you sell it?"

"Why not? Didn't I tell you the Rovers robbed my father of a mine? This isn't a fleabite to what they've got that belongs to us." From the dining room the young rascals passed to the staterooms.

"Trunks full of stuff," observed Flapp. "We shan't fall short of clothing."

"I hope there is money in some of them," answered Dan Baxter.

"Hadn't we better be putting off?" asked Flapp, nervously. "Some of them may be coming back, you know."

"Yes, let us put off at once. This mist that is coming up will help us to get away."

Leaving the stateroom they were in, they went out on deck and began to untie the houseboat. While they were doing so they heard the sounds of two horses approaching.

"Somebody is coming," said Flapp, and an instant later Dora and Nellie came into view. Nellie had her skirt badly torn, and it was her intention, if she could locate the houseboat, to don a new skirt before she returned to where Tom and Dick had left them on the highway.

"It's a pity you fell and tore the skirt," Dora was saying. "But I suppose you can be thankful that you did not hurt yourself."

"That is true. But the boys will think I can't ride, and—Oh!"

Nellie came to a sudden stop and pointed to the houseboat.

"Dan Baxter," burst from Dora's lips. "Oh, how did that fellow get here?"

"Dora Stanhope!" muttered Baxter, and then he and Lew Flapp ran towards the girls.

CHAPTER XXIII
A RUN IN THE DARK

Both girls were thoroughly alarmed by the unexpected appearance of Dan Baxter and his companion and brought their horses to a standstill.

"How do you do, Miss Stanhope?" said Baxter, with a grin.

"What are you doing here?" demanded Dora, icily.

"Oh, nothing much."

"Do you know that that is the Rovers' houseboat?"

"Is it?" said Baxter, in pretended surprise.

"Yes."

"No, I didn't know it." Baxter turned to Nellie. "How are you, Miss Laning? I suppose you are surprised to meet me out here."

"I am," was Nellie's short answer. Both girls wished themselves somewhere else.

"My friend and I were walking down the river when we heard a man on that houseboat calling for help," went on Dan Baxter, glibly. "We went on board and found the captain had fallen down and hurt himself very much. Do you know anything about him?"

"Why, yes!" said Dora, quickly. "It must be Captain Starr!" she added, to Nellie.

"He's in a bad way. If you know him, you had better look after him," continued Dan Baxter.

"I will," and Dora leaped to the ground, followed by Nellie. Both ran towards the houseboat, but at the gang plank they paused.

"I—I think I'll go back and get Dick Rover," said Dora. She did not like the look in Dan Baxter's eyes.

"Yes, and Tom," put in Nellie.

"You shan't go back," roared Dan Baxter. "Go on and help the poor captain."

His manner was so rude that Nellie gave a short, sharp scream—one which reached Tom's ears, as already recorded.

"Don't—don't go on board just yet, Dora," she whispered.

"You shall go on board!" went on Dan Baxter. "Make her go, Flapp. I'll attend to this one," and he caught hold of Dora's arm.

At this both girls screamed—another signal of distress which reached Tom's ears but did no good.

"I don't see the reason—" began Lew Flapp.

"Just do as I say, Flapp. We can make money out of this," answered Dan Baxter.

He caught Dora around the waist and lifted her into the air. She struggled bravely but could do nothing, and in a moment more he had her on the houseboat. Lew Flapp followed with Nellie, who pulled his hair and scratched his face unavailingly.

"Where—where you going to put 'em?" queried Flapp.

"In here," answered Dan Baxter, leading the way to one of the staterooms—that usually occupied by Mrs. Stanhope and Dora. "Now you stay in there and keep quiet, or it will be the worse for you," Baxter went on to the girls.

As Nellie was pushed into the stateroom she fainted and pitched headlong on the floor. Thoroughly alarmed, Dora raised her cousin in her arms. At the same time Baxter shut the door and locked it from the outside.

"Now, don't make a bit of noise, or you'll be sorry for it," he fairly hissed, and his manner was so hateful that Dora was thoroughly cowed.

"What's the next move?" asked Flapp, when he and Baxter were on the outside deck. He was too weak-minded to take a stand and placed himself entirely under the guidance of his companion.

"Get the houseboat away from the shore and be quick about it," was the reply. "Somebody else may be on the way here."

The order to push off was obeyed, and soon the *Dora*, caught by the strong current of the river, was moving down the Ohio and away from the vicinity of Skemport. The mist was now so thick that in a few minutes the shore line was lost entirely to view.

"I must say, I don't like this drifting in the dark," said Flapp. "What if we run into something!"

"We've got to take some risk. I'll light the lanterns as soon as we get a little further away. You stand by with that long pole—in case the houseboat drifts in toward shore again."

The *Dora* had been provided with several long, patent sweeps, and for a while both of the young rascals used these, in an endeavor to get the houseboat out into the middle of the river. In the distance they saw the lights of a steamboat and this was all they had to guide them.

"If we strike good and hard we'll go to the bottom," said Lew Flapp.

"Flapp, you are as nervous as a cat."

"Isn't it true?"

"I don't think so. Most of these boats are built in compartments. If one compartment is smashed the others will keep her afloat."

"Oh, I see." And after that Lew Flapp felt somewhat relieved.

When the houseboat was well away from Skemport, Dan Baxter walked to the door of the stateroom in which Dora and Nellie had been confined.

"Hullo, in there!" he called out.

"What do you want?" asked Dora, timidly.

"How is that other girl, all right?"

"Ye—yes," came from Nellie. "But, oh! Mr. Baxter, what does this mean?"

"Don't grow alarmed. I'm not going to hurt you in the least."

"Yes, but—but—we don't want to go with you."

"I'm sorry, but I can't help that. If we let you go ashore you'll tell the Rovers that we took the houseboat."—"

"And is that why you took us along?" questioned Dora.

"Certainly."

"How far are you going to take us?"

"That depends upon circumstances. I don't know yet where or when we will be able to make a landing."

"It is horrid of you to treat us so."

"Sorry you don't like it, but it can't be helped," answered Dan Baxter, coolly. He paused a moment. "Say, if I unlock that door and let you out will you promise to behave yourselves?"

"What do you mean by that?" questioned Dora.

"I mean will you promise not to scream for help or not to attack myself or Lew Flapp?"

"I shan't promise anything," said Nellie, promptly.

"I don't think I'll promise anything either," joined in her cousin.

"Humph! You had better. It's rather stuffy in that little stateroom."

"We can stand it," answered both.

"All right, suit yourselves. But when you want to come out, let me know."

With these words Dan Baxter walked away, leaving the girls once more to themselves. Both sat down on the edge of a berth, and Nellie placed her head upon Dora's shoulder.

"Oh, Dora, what will become of us?"

"I'm sure I don't know, Nellie."

"They may take us away down the river—miles and miles away!"

"I know that. We must watch our chances and see if we cannot escape."

"Do you think the Rover boys are following the houseboat?"

"Let us hope so."

Thoroughly miserable, the cousins became silent. They felt the houseboat moving swiftly along with the current, but could see nothing on account of the mist and the darkness. Soon they heard the rain coming down.

"It is going to be an awful night," said Dora. "I don't see how anybody could follow this houseboat in such a storm."

Both girls felt like crying, but did their best to hold back the tears. Each was tired out by the doings of the day gone by, but neither thought of going to sleep.

The lanterns had been lit, and both Baxter and Flapp stationed themselves at the front of the houseboat, in an endeavor to pierce the mist. Occasionally they made out some distant light, but could not tell where it belonged.

"We ought to be getting to somewhere pretty soon," remarked Lew Flapp, after a couple of hours had passed. "Don't you think we had better turn her in toward shore?'"

"Not yet, Flapp; we ought to place as much distance as possible between the boat and Skemport. Remember, those Rovers will be after us hot-footed when once they learn the truth of the situation."

"Do you know anything about the river around here?"

"A little, but not much. Do you know anything?"

"No,—I never cared for geography," answered Flapp. "It's getting as black as pitch, and the rain—Hullo, there's another light!"

Flapp pointed to the Kentucky side of the river. Through the mist appeared a dim light, followed by another.

"Wonder if that is the shore or a boat?" mused Baxter.

"Better yell and see."

"Boat, ahoy!"

No answer came back, and for the moment the lights appeared to fade from sight.

"Must have been on shore and we are passing them, Baxter."

"More than likely, and yet—There they are again!"

Dan Baxter was right; the lights had reappeared and now they seemed to approach the houseboat with alarming rapidity.

"They'll run into us if they are not careful," said Flapp, in fresh alarm. "Boat, ahoy!" he screamed. "Keep off!"

"Keep off! Keep off, there!" put in Dan Baxter.

If those in the other craft heard, they paid no attention. The light came closer and closer and of a sudden a fair-sized gasolene launch came into view. She was headed directly for the *Dora*, and a moment later hit the houseboat a telling blow in the side, causing her to careen several feet.

CHAPTER XXIV

61

THE HORSE THIEVES

For the moment it looked as if the houseboat might be sent to the bottom of the Ohio River, and from the stateroom in which the two girls were confined came a loud cry of fright. Dan Baxter and Lew Flapp were also scared, and rushed toward the gasolene launch, not knowing what to do.

"Keep off!"

"Don't sink us!"

Loud cries also came from the launch, and those on the deck of the *Dora* could see several men, wearing raincoats, moving about. The bow of the launch was badly splintered, but otherwise the craft remained undamaged.

"What do you mean by running into us in this fashion?" cried Baxter, seeing that the *Dora* was in no danger of going down.

"Running into you?" came in a rough voice from the launch. "You ran into us!"

"Not much we didn't."

"What boat is that?" came in another voice from the launch.

"A private houseboat. What craft is that?"

"None of your business."

"Thank you." Baxter put on a bold front. "I'm going to report you for running into us, just the same."

"Not much, you won't!" came from the launch. There were a few hurried words spoken in a whisper, and then a boat-hook was thrown on the *Dora* and a man leaped aboard and tied fast.

"Who is in command here?" he demanded, confronting Baxter and Flapp.

"I am," answered Baxter.

"Is she your houseboat?"

"Yes."

"Where are you bound?"

"Down to the Mississippi. But what is that to you?"

"How many of you on board of this craft?" went on the man, ignoring altogether the last question.

"That is my business."

"Well, and I'm going to make it mine," cried the man, and pulled out a revolver. "Answer up, kid; it will be best for you."

He was a burly Kentuckian, all of six feet tall and with a bushy black beard and a breath which smelt strongly of whiskey.

"Don't—don't shoot us!" cried Lew Flapp, in terror. "Don't shoot!"

"I won't—if you'll treat me proper-like," answered the Kentuckian. "How many on board?"

"Four—two young ladies and ourselves," answered Dan Baxter. He was doing some rapid thinking. "Say, perhaps we can strike up a. bargain with you," he went on.

"A bargain? What kind of a bargain?" And the Kentuckian eyed him narrowly.

"We are looking for somebody to tow this houseboat down the river."

At this the Kentuckian gave a loud and brutal laugh.

"Thanks, but I ain't in that ere business."

"All right, then; get aboard of your own boat and we will go on," continued Baxter.

"What's doing up there, Pick?" called another man, from the launch. "Remember, we haven't got all night to waste here."

"That other boat is coming!" cried a third man. "Boys, we are trapped as sure as guns!"

"Not much we ain't," said the Kentuckian who had boarded the houseboat. "Sculley!"

"What next, Pick?"

"You've got a new job. This chap here wants somebody to tow him down the river."

"Well?"

"You start to do the towing, and be quick about it. Hamp, get on board at once! Remember, Sculley, you ain't seen or heard of us, understand?"

"All right, Pick."

The gasolene launch came close once more, and the fellow called Hamp leaped on board. He carried a rifle and was evidently a desperate character.

"See here, I don't understand your game?" began Baxter.

"Didn't you say you wanted somebody to tow you down the river?" asked the fellow addressed as Pick.

"I did, but—"

"Well, Cap'n Sculley of the *Firefly* has taken the job. He'll take you wherever you please, and at your own price. You can't ask for more than that, can you?"

"No, but—"

"I haven't got time to talk, kid—with' that other launch coming after us. I don't know who you are and I reckon you don't know me and my bosom pard here. But let me tell you one thing. It won't be healthy for you to tell anybody that me and my pard are on board here, understand?"

"You are hiding away from somebody?" asked Baxter, quickly.

"I reckon that's the plain United States of it. If you say a word it will go mighty hard with you," and the Kentuckian tapped his revolver.

"You can trust us," replied Baxter, promptly. "Tell me what you want done and I'll agree to do it."

"You will?" The Kentuckian eyed him more closely than ever. "Say, you can't play any game on me,—I'm too old for it."

"I shan't play any game on you. Just say what you want done and I'll help you all I can—providing that launch takes us down the river as quick as it can."

"Ha! Maybe you want to get away, too, eh?"

"I want to get down the river, yes. Perhaps I'll tell you more,—after I am certain I can trust you," added Baxter, significantly.

"Good enough, I'll go you. If that other launch comes up, tell 'em anything but that you have strangers on board, or that you have seen us."

"I will."

"If you play us foul—"

"I shan't play you foul, so don't worry."

By this time the second launch was coming up through the mist and the two men from Kentucky retired to the cabin of the houseboat. In the meantime the first launch had tied fast to the *Dora* and was beginning to tow the houseboat down the stream.

"Boat, ahoy, there!" was the call.

"Ahoy!" answered the man on the first launch.

"Got any passengers on board?"

"No."

"What's your tow?"

"A houseboat."

"Who is on board?"

"I don't know exactly. What do you want to know for?"

"We are looking for a couple of horse thieves who ran away from Kepples about two hours ago."

"I haven't seen anything of any horse thieves."

The second launch now came up to the houseboat. As may be surmised Dan Baxter and Lew Flapp had listened to the talk with keen interest.

"Those chaps are horse thieves," muttered Flapp.

"Yes,—but don't open your mouth, Flapp," answered the leader of the evil-doers.

63

"Houseboat, ahoy!" was the call.

"Hullo, the launch," answered Baxter.

"Seen anything of any strangers within the past two hours?"

"Strangers?" repeated Baxter. "Yes, I did."

"Where?"

"About a mile back. Two men in a small sailboat, beating up the river."

"How were they dressed?"

"In raincoats. One was a tall fellow with a heavy beard."

"That's our game, Curly!" was the exclamation on the second launch. "About a mile up the river, you say?"

"About that—or maybe a mile and a half," replied Dan Baxter.

"Thank you. We'll get after them now!" And in a moment more the second launch sheered off and started up the Ohio through the mist and rain.

As soon as it was out of sight the men in the cabin of the *Dora* came out again.

"That was well done, kid," cried he called Pick. "And it was well you did it that way. If you had said we were aboard you might have got a dose of lead in your head."

"I always keep my word," replied Baxter.

"You're a game young rooster, and I reckon I can't call you kid no more. What's your handle?"

"What's yours?"

"Pick Loring."

"You're a horse thief, it seems."

"I don't deny it."

"My name is Dan Baxter, and this is my friend, Lew Flapp."

"Glad to know you. This is my pard in business, Hamp Gouch. We had to quit in a hurry, but I reckon we fell in the right hands," and Pick Loring closed one eye suggestively and questioningly.

"You're safe with us, Loring,—if you'll give us a lift."

"I always stick to them as sticks to me."

"If you want to stay on this houseboat for a while you can do it."

"We'll have to stay on this craft. It's about the only place we'll be safe—for a day or two at least."

"You can stay a couple of weeks, if you want to—all providing you'll lend us your assistance."

"It's a go. Now what's your game? You must have one, or you wouldn't act in this style," said Pick Loring.

CHAPTER XXV
PLOTTING AGAINST DORA AND NELLIE

"In the first place," said Dan Baxter, "perhaps we had better give some directions to that man on the launch."

"What kind of directions?"

"We want to go straight down the river for the present."

"He'll take you down. I told him not to go near either shore."

"Is he to be trusted?"

"Sure. He'll do anything I tell him to."

"Very well, then, that is settled. In the second place, tell me if I am right. You are both wanted for stealing sixteen horses over at a place called Kepples."

"Who told you we took sixteen horses?"

"I read about it in the papers a couple of days ago."

"Well, the report is true. I don't deny it."

"You were fleeing from the officers of the law."

"That's as straight as shooting," came from Hamp Gouch.

"If we help you to escape, will you stick by us in a little game we are trying to put through?"

64

"I will," answered Pick Loring, promptly.

"So will I," added Hamp Gouch. "No game too daring for me either."

"Well, it's this way," continued Dan Baxter. "Supposing I told you I had a game on that beats horse stealing all to bits. Would you go in for half of what was in it?"

"Sure."

"Trust me," added Gouch. "Say," he went on. "Got any liquor aboard? This rain is beastly."

"I guess there is some liquor. We'll hunt around and see."

"Ha!" exclaimed Pick Loring. "Say, perhaps you don't know much more about this houseboat than we did about them horses we took."

"As you just said, I don't deny it."

"You and your pard are running off with the boat?" queried Hamp Gouch.

"Yes."

"Good enough. We claim a half-interest in the boat. Don't that go?"

"That's pretty cheeky," returned Lew Flapp.

"Let it go at that, Flapp," came from Baxter. "Yes, you can have a half-interest. But that isn't our game."

"What is the game?"

"On board of this houseboat are two girls who are mighty anxious to get back to their families and friends."

"Run off with 'em, did you?" cried Pick Loring, and now it must be confessed that he was really astonished.

"We carried them off, yes. And we don't expect to let them get back home unless we can make considerable money out of it," continued Dan Baxter.

"Are they rich?"

"They are fairly well-to-do, and they have close personal friends who, I feel sure, would pay a good price to see the girls get home again unharmed."

"You're putty young to be runnin' a game like this," came from Hamp Gouch.

"Maybe, but I know just what I am doing."

They walked into the living room, and Lew Flapp made an inspection of the pantry and then of Captain Starr's private apartment. As it happened, the captain used liquor, and several bottles were brought out, much to the satisfaction of the horse thieves.

"This makes me feel more like talking," said Hamp Gouch, after swallowing a goodly portion of the stuff.

"Perhaps you had better give us the whole game straight from start to now," said Pick Loring. "Then we can make up our minds just what we can do."

Sitting down, Dan Baxter told as much of himself and Lew Flapp as he deemed necessary, and told about the trip on the houseboat which the Rovers, Stanhopes, and the Lanings had been taking. Then he told how Dora and Nellie had been abducted and how the voyage down the Ohio had been started in the mist and the darkness.

"You're a putty bold pair for your years," said Pick Loring. "Hang me if I don't admire you!" And he smiled in his coarse way.

"Of course you can see the possibilities in this," went on Dan Baxter. "Supposing we can make the Stanhopes and Lanings and Rovers pay over fifty or sixty thousand dollars for the return of the girls. That means a nice sum for each of us."

"Right you are," came from Hamp Gouch. "As you say, it beats horse stealing."

"Have they got the money?" asked the other Kentuckian.

"They have a good deal more than that between them. The Rovers are very rich."

"But they are only friends?"

"More than that. Dick Rover is very sweet on Dora Stanhope, and Tom Rover thinks the world of Nellie Laning."

65

"Then of course they'll help pay up—especially if they hear the girls are likely to suffer. We can write to 'em and say we'll starve the girls to death if the money don't come our way."

"Exactly. But we've got to find some place to hide first. We can't stay on the river any great length of time. They'll send word about the houseboat from one town to another and the authorities will be on the lookout for us."

"I know where you can take this houseboat," put in Hamp Gouch. "Up Shaggam Creek. There is a dandy hiding place there and nobody around but old Jake Shaggam, and we can easily 'buy him off, so as he won't open his mouth."

"How far is that creek from here?"

"About thirty-five miles."

The matter was talked over for fully an hour, and it was at last decided that the houseboat should go up Shaggam Creek, at least for the time being. If that place got too hot to hold them they could move further down the river during the nights to follow.

The man on the launch was called up and matters were explained to him by Pick Loring.

"Sculley is a good fellow," said Loring to Baxter. "He will do whatever I say and take whatever I give him,—and keep his mouth shut."

"That's the kind of a follower to have," was Baxter's answer.

The horse thieves were hungry, and a fire was started in the galley of the houseboat. The men cooked themselves something to eat and Baxter and Flapp did the same. It must be confessed that Flapp did not like the newcomers and hated to have anything to do with them. But he was too much of a coward to speak up, and so did as Baxter dictated. Thus is one rascal held under the thumb of another. It was only when Lew Flapp was among those who were smaller and weaker than himself that he dared to play the part of the bully.

Dora and Nellie heard the loud talking after the crashing of the launch into the houseboat and also heard part of what followed. Both wanted to cry out for assistance, but did not dare, fearing that something still worse might happen to them.

"They might bind and gag us," said Nellie. "That Dan Baxter is bad enough to do almost anything."

"Yes, and from the way Lew Flapp treated Dick, I should think he was almost as wicked as Baxter," answered her cousin.

The girls wondered who the newcomers on board could be, but had no means of finding out. Nobody came near them, and at last tired nature asserted itself and both dropped into a troublous doze.

When they awoke it was still dark. A steam whistle had aroused them. They looked out of the stateroom window. It had stopped raining, but the mist was just as thick as ever.

"Oh, if only it would clear up!" sighed Dora. "Nobody will be able to follow the houseboat in such a mist as this."

"Where do you think they will take us, Dora?" questioned Nellie.

"Goodness only knows. Perhaps down the Mississippi, or maybe to the Gulf of Mexico."

"Oh, Dora, would they dare to do that?" And Nellie's face grew pale.

Dora shrugged her shoulders by way of reply, and for the time being the cousins relapsed into silence. Both were thinking of their mothers and of the Rovers. What had the others said to their strange disappearance?

"It is perfectly dreadful!" cried Nellie, at last, and burst into tears, and Dora followed. The crying appeared to do them some good and after half an hour they became more at ease.

"We must escape if we possibly can, Nellie," said Dora. "We cannot afford to remain a moment longer on this houseboat than is necessary."

"But how are we going to escape? It looks to me as if we were out in the middle of the river."

"That is true. But both of us can row, and there is a small rowboat on board. If we could launch that and get away we might escape."

"Well, I am willing to try it, if you think it can be done. But we must get out of this stateroom first."

The two girls listened, but nobody appeared to be anywhere near them.

"I can hear them talking in the kitchen," said Nellie. "More than likely they are getting something to eat."

"I could eat something myself."

"So could I. But I'd rather get away."

Both looked for some means of getting out of the stateroom and suddenly Dora uttered a cry of delight.

"Oh, why didn't I think of it before!"

"Think of what?"

"That key on the hook over there. It fits the door."

"Then we can get out!"

"If that other key isn't on the outside."

Dora got down and looked through the keyhole. It was clear and she quickly inserted the key taken from the hook. It fitted perfectly, and in a second more the door was unlocked.

"Wait,—until I make sure that nobody is around!" whispered Dora. She was so agitated she could scarcely speak.

She opened the door cautiously and looked out. Not a soul was in sight. From the galley came a steady hum of voices and a rattle of pots and dishes.

"They are too busy to watch us just now—the way is clear," she whispered. "Come on."

"Let us lock the door behind us, and stuff the keyhole," answered Nellie. "Then they will think we are inside and won't answer."

This was done, and with their hearts beating wildly the two girls stole to the end of the houseboat, where lay the small rowboat Dora had mentioned.

CHAPTER XXVI

THE SEARCH ON THE RIVER

As may be surmised, the news which Dick and Tom had to tell to the others at the stock farm produced great excitement.

"Dora and Nellie gone!" gasped Mrs. Stanhope. "Oh, Dick, what has become of them?"

"They must have gotten into some trouble!" cried Mrs. Laning. "You found no trace of them?"

"We did not," said Tom. "But we tried hard enough, I can assure you."

"Oh, what shall we do?" wailed Mrs. Stanhope, and then she fainted away, and it was a good quarter of an hour before she could be restored.

All the boys were highly excited, and Sam was for making a search for the missing houseboat without delay.

"They may have gone on board and Captain Starr may have sailed off with them," said the youngest Rover. "Remember, he is a queer stick, to say the least."

"That doesn't explain the screams I heard," said Tom.

"I dink me dot Paxter got somedings to do mit dis," said Hans. "He vos a rascals from his hair to his doenails alretty!"

"The only thing to do is to make a search," came from Songbird Powell. "I'm ready to go out, rain or no rain."

They were all ready, and in the end it was decided that all of the boys should prosecute the hunt, leaving Mrs. Stanhope, Mrs. Laning, and Grace with the wife of the proprietor of the stock farm. The proprietor himself, a Kentuckian named Paul Livingstone, said he would go with them.

"If there has been foul play of any sort I will aid you to have justice done," said Paul Livingstone. "To me this whole thing looks mightily crooked."

"One thing is certain,—if the houseboat was stolen, the mist and rain will aid the thieves to get away with her," said Dick.

It was a rather silent crowd that rode into Skemport an hour and a half later. Here a doctor was roused up and sent to the stock farm, to see if Mrs. Stanhope needed him, for she was weak and might collapse completely when least expected.

Once at the spot where the *Dora* had been tied up, another search was begun for the girls and the houseboat. Some went up the shore and others down, each with a lantern which had been provided to dispel the gloom.

"Oh, where? Oh, where?

In dire despair

We search the shore in vain!"

came lowly from Songbird, but then he felt too heavy-hearted to finish the verse and heaved a sigh instead. "This is simply heart-rending," he said.

"That's what it is," answered Dick.

Hans was not far off, shambling along in his own peculiar fashion. He held up his lantern and by the dim rays made out a building some distance away.

"I yonder vot is in dare?" he said to himself. "Maype I go und look, hey? It ton't cost me noddings."

Through the mist and rain he approached the building and walked around to the door, which was closed. He flung it open and held up his lantern to see inside.

"*Du meine Zeit!* Vot is dis?" he gasped. "Cabtain Starr, or I vos treaming! Hi, Cabtain, vot you vos doing here, alretty?" he called out.

"Is that—that you, Mueller?" asked the captain, in a trembling voice.

"Sure it vos me. Vot you did here, tole me dot?"

"I—the rascals tied me fast. They said they'd come and give me a hundred dollars in the morning, but I don't think they'll do it."

"Py chimanatics! Vait a minute." Hans ran outside and waved his lantern. "Come here!" he bawled. "Come here, kvick, eferybody!"

His cry summoned the others, and they quickly gathered at the stable and released the captain. While they were doing this, they made the simple-minded fellow tell his story.

"Describe those two fellows," said Dick, and Captain Starr did so.

The description was perfect.

"Dan Baxter and Lew Flapp!" cried Tom.

"Of course, you didn't send that message?" asked the captain, of Dick.

"I did not, captain. It was a trick to get you away from the *Dora* and steal the houseboat."

"Is the craft stolen?"

"Yes."

"Oh, dear!" Captain Starr wrung his hands. "Please don't blame me!"

"I don't know as I can blame you, exactly. But you want to have your wits about you after this."

When Captain Starr heard about the disappearance of the two girls he was more interested than ever.

"I heard them scream," he said.

"Where was that?"

"I think they must have been right in front of where the *Dora* was tied up."

"When was this?" asked Sam.

"Not very long after the villains made me their prisoner."

"It's as clear as day!" cried Fred Garrison. "Baxter and Flapp first stole the houseboat and then they abducted Dora and Nellie."

"It's a wretched piece of business," came from Dick. "Oh, if I can only lay my hands on them they shall suffer for it!"

"We must chase the houseboat, that's all I know to do," put in Tom. "And the quicker we begin the better."

"That's easily said, Tom. How are we going to locate the craft in this mist? She may have gone up the stream and she may have gone down."

"More than likely she went down with the current. They hadn't any steam tug handy to pull her."

Paul Livingstone was appealed to and told them where they could find the coal docks at which their own tug was lying. All hurried to the place and called up Captain Carson.

"I'll get up steam just as soon as I can," said the tug captain, and hustled out his engineer and fireman. Soon the black smoke was pouring from the tug's stack and in less than half an hour they were ready to move.

"This seems like a wild-goose chase," remarked Sam. "But it is better than standing around with one's hands in his pockets."

"I wish I had dat Dan Baxter heah!" said Aleck Pop. "I'd duck him in the ribber an' hold him undah 'bout ten minutes!"

All were soon on the steam tug, which was crowded by the party. The lanterns were lit, and they moved down the Ohio slowly and cautiously.

"We had better move from side to side of the river," suggested Dick. "Then we won't be so liable to pass the houseboat without seeing her."

As all of the party were wet, they took turns in drying and warming themselves in the engine-room of the tug. Those on the lookout did what they could to pierce the gloom, but with small satisfaction.

Half an hour later they passed a small river steamer and hailed the craft.

"What's wanted?" shouted somebody through a megaphone.

"Seen anything of a houseboat around here?"

"No," was the prompt answer.

"All right; thanks!" And then they allowed the river steamer to pass them.

"Dis night vos so vet like neffer vos!" remarked Hans.

"Well, we have got to make the best of it," answered Dick. "I don't care how wet I get, if only we are successful in our chase."

"I am mit you on dot," returned the German cadet, quickly.

Two hours passed and they saw no other craft. They had passed several settlements of more or less importance, but not a sign of the missing houseboat appeared.

"Here comes something!" cried Tom, presently, as they heard a distant puff-puff.

"Steer in the direction of that sound," said Dick, to Captain Carson, and this was done.

Out of the mist appeared the light of a long launch, having on board several officers of the law.

"Steam tug, ahoy!" was the cry.

"Ahoy!" shouted back Captain Carson.

"Seen anything of another launch around here?"

"No."

"See anything of a small sailboat?"

"No."

"Confound the luck!" came in another voice from the launch.

"What's the matter?" asked Paul Livingstone.

"Hullo, Mr. Livingstone, is that you?" called out one of the officers of the law on the launch.

"It is, Captain Dixon. What's the trouble?"

"We are looking for those two horse thieves, Pick Loring and Hamp Gouch. I suppose you know they escaped."

"So I heard. Well, I hope you get them," answered the owner of the stock farm. "They took four of my horses once."

"So I understand. What are you doing out here this time of night?"

"We are looking for a houseboat that was stolen. Seen anything of such a craft?"

"Certainly we did."

"You did!" burst from Dick and several of the others. "Where?"

"Down the river four or five miles. The fellows on board told us that they had seen a sailboat with two men in it beating up the river, and from the description we took the men to be Loring and Gouch."

"How did the houseboat look?" asked Tom.

One of the officers of the law gave a brief description of the *Dora* and told what he could of Baxter and Flapp.

"It's our houseboat beyond a doubt," said Sam. "And those two fellows were Flapp and Baxter."

"Did you see anybody else on the houseboat?" questioned Dick.

"Not a soul. So the houseboat was stolen?" went on the police officer, curiously.

"Yes, and, worse than that, two girls have been abducted."

"Creation! That's serious."

"It will be serious for those rascals if we catch them!" muttered Tom. "Where did the houseboat go to?"

"It was heading straight down the river when we saw it last."

"Then come!" cried Dick. "Let us go after the craft and lose no time."

A moment later the steam tug parted company with the launch, and the chase after the *Dora* was resumed.

CHAPTER XXVII
CAUGHT ONCE MORE

The two girls hardly dared to breathe as they stood at the rear of the houseboat, trying to untie the small rowboat which lay on the deck.

"Oh, Dora, supposing they find us out?" gasped Nellie.

"I don't think we'll be any worse off than we were," answered her cousin.

"Do you think we can launch the rowboat and get into it without upsetting?"

"We can try."

The small craft was soon unfastened and they dragged it to the edge of the houseboat. There was a small slide, on hinges, and they had seen the boys use this more than once, and knew how it worked. Down went the rowboat with a slight splash, and they hauled the craft up close by aid of the rope attached to the bow.

"Now the oars!" whispered Dora.

They were at hand, in a rack at the back of the dining room, and soon she had secured two pairs.

"You drop in first, Nellie," went on Dora. "Be quick, but don't fall overboard."

Nellie obeyed, trembling in every limb. She landed safely and in a few seconds Dora followed. Just as this was done a man appeared on the deck of the houseboat, followed by another.

"Oh, Dora—" began Nellie, when her cousin silenced her. Then the rope was untied, and the rowboat was allowed to drift astern of the larger craft.

"Hullo, there!" came suddenly out of the darkness. "What's up back there?"

"Who are you calling to, Hamp?" came from the galley.

"Something doing back here," answered Hamp Gouch. "Somebody just cut loose from our stern."

"What's that?" burst out Dan Baxter, and tumbled out on deck, followed by the others.

70

"I said somebody just cut loose from this houseboat. There they go," and the horse thief pointed with his hand.

"It can't be the girls!" cried Flapp.

"Run to the stateroom and see," answered Baxter. "I'll get the big lantern."

Lew Flapp hurried to the door of the state-room, taking with him the key Baxter handed over.

"Hullo, in there!" he shouted. "Are you awake?"

Receiving no answer he knocked loudly on the door.

"I say, why don't you answer?" he went on. "I'm coming in."

Still receiving no reply, he started to put the key in the lock and found that he could not do so.

"It won't do any good to block the lock," he called out. "Answer me, or I'll break down the door."

Still nothing but silence, and in perplexity he ran back to Baxter.

"I can't get a sound out of them, and the keyhole is stuffed," he said.

"We'll break in the door," said the leader of the evil-doers.

It took but a minute to execute this threat, for the door was thin and frail. Both gave a hasty look around.

"Gone!"

"They must have taken the rowboat and rowed away," said Lew Flapp.

Both went back to where they had left Pick Loring and Hamp Gouch.

"The girls are gone," said Baxter. "They must have skipped in that rowboat."

"We can soon fix 'em," muttered Loring. "We'll get Sculley to go after them."

The launch ahead was signaled and soon came up alongside.

"What's wanted now?"

"Take me aboard and I'll tell you," answered Baxter, and he and Pick Loring boarded the launch.

In the meantime the two girls had placed the oars into the rowlocks and were rowing off as fast as their strength would permit.

"Oh, Dora, do you think we can get away!" gasped Nellie.

"We must! Do your best, and keep time with me."

"But which way are we going?"

"I don't know, yet. The best we can do is to keep away from the lights of the houseboat."

Stroke after stroke was taken in dire desperation, and after a while they had the satisfaction of seeing the lights of the houseboat fading away in the distance.

All was gloom and mist around them and they stopped rowing, not knowing in which direction to turn next.

"We are lost on the river," said Nellie.

"Yes, but that is better than being in the hands of our enemies," was Dora's answer.

"Yes, Dora, ten times over. But what shall we do next?"

"Let us try to row crosswise with the current. That is sure to bring us to shore sooner or later."

This they set out to do, and after a while felt certain that they were drawing close to the river bank on the north.

"We are getting there!" cried Nellie. "Oh, Dora, aren't you glad?"

Scarcely had she spoken when they saw a light behind them, and a long launch came unexpectedly into view. In the bow stood Dan Baxter with a lantern.

"I thought I heard their oars," cried that rascal. "Here they are!"

"Pull, pull, Nellie!" cried Dora. "Pull, or we shall be captured!"

Both of the girls rowed with all their strength, but before they could gain the shore, which was now less than two rods away, the launch came up and made fast to the rowboat.

71

"Might as well give it up," said Dan Baxter, sarcastically. "It's no use, as you can see."

"Oh, Mr. Baxter, do let us go!" pleaded Nellie, more terrorized than ever before.

"Not much! You have got to go back to the houseboat."

At this Nellie gave a loud scream, and Dora immediately followed with a prolonged call for help.

"Shut them up!" came from Pick Loring. "There are a whole lot of people living around here."

Without answering, Dan Baxter leaped into the rowboat and took Dora by the arm roughly.

"If you don't shut up, I'll gag you!" he cried.

"Let me go!" she said, and struck at him feebly. While this was going on Pick Loring came over and took hold of Nellie.

"Tow us along, Sculley!" called the horse thief. "Get back to the houseboat as soon as you can."

"What's the matter out there?" came in an unexpected call from the shore. The speaker could not be seen.

"Help us!" shrieked Dora. "We are two girls and some men are carrying us off."

"You don't say so!" ejaculated the speaker on shore.

"Tell the Rover boys!" called out Nellie. "Dan Baxter is taking us down the river on the houseboat."

"Save us, and we will pay you well," added Dora, and then Baxter's not over cleanly hand was clapped over her mouth, and she could say no more. Loring's hand was likewise placed over Nellie's mouth, and then the launch began to tow the rowboat back into midstream once more.

The poor girls were utterly disheartened and dropped back on the seats in something close to a faint.

"This is a mess," growled Dan Baxter. "Have you any idea who that was that called from the shore?"

"Some kind of a watchman," answered Loring. "We have got to get out of this neighborhood in railroad time or the jig's up," he added.

"Well, I'm willing."

It did not take long to catch up to the houseboat, which was drifting down the river in the fashion it had pursued before being towed by the Lunch. Flapp and Hamp Gouch were waiting impatiently on the deck.

"Got 'em?" asked Lew Flapp.

"Yes, but we had no time to spare," returned Dan Baxter. "Two minutes more and they would have been ashore."

"After this maybe we had better stand guard over them, Baxter."

"Just what I have been thinking."

Once alongside of the houseboat, the two girls were forced on board once more and taken to the stateroom next to that which they had before occupied.

The window was locked up and nailed and after the girls were inside, Dan Baxter placed a strong bolt outside.

"Now if you try to escape again you may get hurt," he called out, after the job was done.

"Mr. Baxter, you shall suffer for this!" answered Dora, as spiritedly as she could.

"Oh, don't think you can scare me."

"The Rovers will get on your track soon."

"I am not afraid of them."

"You said that before, but you've always been glad enough to hide from them."

"It's false!" cried Baxter, in a passion. "I never hid from them."

"You are hiding now. You dare not face them openly."

"Oh, give us a rest. I am doing this for the money that is in it."

"Money?"

"Yes, money."

"I do not understand you."

"Well, you'll understand to-morrow or the day after."

"We haven't any money to give you," put in Nellie.

"No, but maybe your folks have."

"Are you going to make them pay you for releasing us?"

"That's it."

"Perhaps they won't pay," said Dora.

"If they don't, so much the worse for you. But I know they'll pay—and so will the Rovers pay," chuckled Baxter.

"What have the Rovers to do with it? Or perhaps you want them to pay you for giving back the houseboat."

"They'll pay for both—for the houseboat and for releasing you. I know Dick and Tom Rover won't want to see you remain in the power of me and Flapp and our friends."

"Dan Baxter, you are a villain!" burst out both girls.

"Thank you for the compliment," returned the rascal, coolly. "I hope you'll enjoy your stay in that stateroom."

"You ought to be in prison!" went on Dora.

"If you talk that way you'll get no breakfast in the morning."

"I don't want any of your breakfast!" and Dora stamped her foot to show she meant it.

"Oh, you'll sing a different tune when you get good and hungry," growled Dan Baxter, and he walked away, leaving the girls once more to themselves.

CHAPTER XXVIII

A MESSSAGE FOR THE ROVERS

Morning found the Rovers and their friends still on the steam launch, looking in all directions for the houseboat.

The rain had ceased and there was every indication that the mist would blow away by noon, but at present it was hard to see a hundred feet in any direction.

"Nature has assisted them to escape," said Dick, bitterly.

"Oh, we'll find them sooner or later," answered Sam.

"Perhaps, Sam. But think of how the girls may be suffering in the meantime."

"I know; and Mrs. Stanhope and Mrs. Laning are suffering too."

The steam tug carried only a small stock of provisions, and it was decided to go ashore at a small place called Gridley's for breakfast. Here there was a country hotel at which they obtained a breakfast which put all in a slightly better physical condition.

The proprietor of the hotel was a bit curious to learn the cause of their unexpected appearance and became interested when Dick told him about the missing houseboat.

"Wonder if that had anything to do with a story Bill Daws told me an hour ago," said he. "Bill works at the mill clown by the river. Last night, in the dark and mist, he heard somebody in a rowboat and a launch having a row. Two gals screamed for help, and somebody said something about a houseboat and tell somebody something—he couldn't tell exactly what. I thought Bill had 'em on, but maybe he didn't."

"Where is this Bill Daws now?" asked Dick.

"Gone home. He works nights and sleeps in the daytime."

"Where does he live?"

"Just up that street over yonder—in the square stone house with the red barn back of it."

Waiting to hear no more, Dick set off for the house mentioned, taking Tom with him. They rapped loudly on the door and an elderly woman answered their summons.

"Is Mr. Bill Daws in?" asked Dick.

"Yes, sir, but he has gone to bed."

"I must speak to him a minute. Tell him it's about the talking he heard on the river in the dark."

"Oh, is that so! He told me something about it," answered the woman.

She went off and coming back invited them into the house. Soon Bill Daws appeared, having slipped on part of his clothing.

"I can't tell ye a great deal," said the watchman. "I heard two gals cry out and some men was trying to shet 'em up. One gal said something about a houseboat and about telling somebody about it."

"Did she say to tell the Rovers?"

"Thet's it! Thet's it! I couldn't think o' thet name nohow, but now you hev struck it fust clip."

"The girls were trying to escape in the rowboat?"

"I reckon so, and the men in the launch were after 'em."

"Where did they go?"

"Out into the river, and thet's the last I see or heard o' 'em."

"Thank you," answered Dick, and seeing that Bill Daws was poor he gave the fellow two dollars, for which the watchman was profoundly grateful.

"It proves one thing," said Tom, when the brothers were coming away. "We are on the right track."

"Right you are, Tom. I hope we stay on the trail until we run down our quarry."

Not long after this the entire party was on the steam launch once more. They took with them provisions enough to last a couple of days and also an extra cask of drinking water.

By one o'clock in the afternoon the sun burst through the mist and an hour later the entire river was clear, so that they could see steamboats and sailboats a long distance off. The captain of the tug brought forth his spyglass and they took turns in looking through the instrument.

"Nothing like a houseboat in sight," said Sam, disconsolately. "It beats the nation where they have gone to."

"They may be hiding around some point or in some cove," suggested Fred. "They must know that we will follow them."

"I think you ought to telegraph up and down the river," put in Songbird.

"Dot's der dalk," came from Hans. "Let eferypody know vot rascals da vos alretty!"

In the middle of the afternoon they made a stop at a town called Smuggs' Landing and from this point Dick sent messages in various directions. One message was sent to a city ten miles further down the river and an answer came back in half an hour stating that, so far as the authorities could find out, nothing had been seen of the *Dora*.

"Now the question is, has she gone past that town, or is she between there and this point?" said Dick.

"Persackly," came from Aleck. "An' I dun gib two dollahs to know de answer to dat cojumdrum."

"All we can do is to continue the search," said Tom. "But I must say it is getting a good deal like looking for a needle in a haystack."

"Vot for you looks for a needle py a haystack?" questioned Hans, innocently. "Needles ton't vos goot for noddings in hay. A hoss vot schwallows a needle vould die kvick, I tole you dot!" And his innocence brought forth a short laugh.

"I move we make a swift run down the river for a distance of twenty or thirty miles," came from Tom. "We can go down on one side and come up the other, and keep the spyglass handy, so that nothing that can be seen escapes us."

The matter was discussed a few minutes and it was decided to follow Tom's suggestion. Additional coal had been taken on and soon the steam tug was flying down the river under a full head of steam, causing not a little spray to fly over the forward deck.

"Say, dot pow ist like a fountain," was Hans' comment, after he had received an unexpected ducking. "I shall sit py der pack deck after dis;" and he did.

So far Captain Starr had said but little during the pursuit, but now he began to show signs of interest.

"Let me lay my hands on the villains who tied me fast in that stable and I shall teach them a lesson they will not forget in a hurry," said he, bitterly. "They made a fool of me."

"That's what they did, captain," said Sam. "Still, they might have imposed upon anybody."

"I've been thinking of something. You'll remember about those two horse thieves?" went on the captain of the houseboat.

"To be sure."

"Couldn't it be possible that they got on the *Dora* too?"

"It's possible." Sam mused for a moment. "That sailboat story might have been a fake."

He called Dick and Mr. Livingstone to him and repeated what Captain Starr had said.

"Such a thing is possible," said Dick. "But we have no proofs."

"If we can catch those thieves as well as Baxter and Flapp it will be a good job done," said the owner of the stock farm. And from that moment he took a greater interest in the pursuit than ever.

Night came on and still they saw nothing of the houseboat. They had gone down the river a distance of twenty miles and were now on their way back.

"We've missed them," said Dick, soberly.

"It certainly looks like it," returned Tom. Every bit of fun had gone out of him. "It's rough, isn't it?"

"I'm thinking of what to telegraph to Mrs. Stanhope and Mrs. Laning," went on the eldest Rover. "I hate to send bad news."

"Tell them you are still following the houseboat and that you know Dora and Nellie are on board. It's the best we can do." And when they landed a message was sent to that effect. Soon a message came back, which read as follows:

"Bring them back safe and sound, no matter what the cost."

"We will, if it can be done," muttered Dick, and clenched his fists with a determination that meant a great deal.

The night was spent at a hotel in one of the small towns, and at daylight the search for the missing houseboat was renewed. It had been decided to drop down the Ohio further than ever, and look into every smaller stream they came to by the way.

Thus several hours passed, when they found themselves on the south side of the river, not far from the entrance to a good-sized creek.

Down the stream came a worn and battered rowboat in which was seated an old man dressed in rags. As he approached the steam tug he stopped rowing.

"Say," he drawled. "Kin you-uns tell me whar to find a party called the Rovers?"

"That's our party right here," replied Dick, and he added, excitedly: "What do you want to know for?"

"So you-uns are really the Rovers?"

"Yes."

"Searching fer somebody?"

"Yes,—two young ladies."

"Good 'nough. Got a message for ye."

And the old man rowed toward the steam launch once more.

CHAPTER XXIX
JAKE SHAGGAM, OF SHAGGAM CREEK

"They will watch us more closely than ever now," said Dora, after she and her cousin were left to themselves in the stateroom on board of the houseboat.

"I presume that is true," answered Nellie, gloomily.

"They expect to make money by carrying us off, Nellie."

"I don't see how they can do it. Papa hasn't much money to pay over to them, and won't have, unless he sells the farm."

"Mamma has quite some money of mine," went on Dora. "Perhaps they will make her pay over that. And then they are going to try to get something out of the Rovers too."

"It's a shame!"

"They ought not to have a cent!"

The girls sat down and talked the matter over until daylight. At about nine o'clock Lew Flapp approached the stateroom door.

"Don't you want something to eat?" he asked, civilly.

"I want a drink," answered Nellie, promptly, for she was exceedingly thirsty.

"I've got a pitcher of ice water for you and some breakfast, too. You might as well eat it as not. There's no sense in starving yourselves."

"I suppose that is true," whispered Nellie to her cousin. She was hungry as well as thirsty, having had no supper the night before.

The door was opened and Lew Flapp passed the food and drink into them. Then he stood in the doorway eyeing them curiously.

"It's too bad you won't be friends with us," said he, with a grin. "It would be much pleasanter to be friends."

"Thank you, but I don't want you for a friend, Mr. Flapp," said Dora, frigidly.

"I ain't so bad as you think I am."

"You are bad enough."

"I ain't bad at all. Dick Rover got me in a scrape at school, and ever since that time he's been spreading evil reports about me."

"You robbed that jewelry store."

"No, I didn't, and I can prove it. The Rovers were the real thieves."

"You cannot make us believe such .a tale. We know the Rovers too well," said Dora, warmly.

"They are as honest as any boys can be," added Nellie.

"Bah! You do not know what you are talking about. They are crafty, that is all,— and half the cadets at Putnam Hall know it."

To this neither of the girls would reply. They wished to close the stateroom door, but Lew Flapp held it open.

"I think you might give me a kiss for bringing you the eating," he said, with another grin.

"I'll give you—this!" answered Dora, and pushed the door shut in his face. There happened to be a bolt on the inside and she quickly shoved it into place.

"Just you wait—I'll get square on you!" growled Lew Flapp, from the outside, and then they heard him stamp off, very much out of sorts.

Fortunately for the girls, the breakfast brought to them was quite fair and there was plenty of it. They ate sparingly, resolved to save what was left until later in the day.

"He may not bring us anything more," said Dora. "Perhaps I did wrong to shut the door on his nose."

"You did just right, Dora," answered her cousin, promptly. "I think he and Baxter are horrid!"

"But they have us in their power, and have some men to aid them, too!"

"I wonder who those men can be?"

"I do not know, but they are very rough. I suppose they would do almost anything for money. They smell strongly of liquor."

Slowly the time went by. They tried to look out of the stateroom window, but Dan Baxter had placed a bit of canvas outside in such a position that they could see nothing.

"They do not want us to find out where they are taking us," said Dora, and her surmise was correct.

76

Night was coming on once more when they felt a sudden jar of the houseboat, followed by several other jars. Then they heard a scraping and a scratching.

"We have struck the bottom and are scraping along some trees and bushes," said Nellie. "Where can we be?"

"Here is a fine shelter!" they heard Pick Loring exclaim. "They'll never spot the houseboat in such a cove as this."

"I believe you," answered Dan Baxter. "It is certainly a dandy hiding place."

"Those girls can't very well get ashore neither," said Hamp Gouch. "If they tried it they would get into mud up to their waists."

"Is this Shaggam Creek—the place you spoke about?" asked Lew Flapp.

"Yes."

"You said there was an old man around here named Jake Shaggam."

"Yes, he lives in that tumble-down shanty over the hill. I don't think he will bother us."

"Does he live there alone?"

"Yes. He is a bachelor and don't like to go down to the village."

The girls heard this talk quite plainly, but presently Baxter, Flapp, and the two horse thieves withdrew to another part of the houseboat and they heard no more.

"We are at a place called Shaggam Creek," said Dora. "That is worth remembering."

"If only we could get some sort of a message to the Rover boys and the others," sighed Nellie. "Dora, can't we manage it somehow?"

"Perhaps we can—anyway, it won't do any harm to write out a message or two, so as to have them ready to send off if the opportunity shows itself."

Paper and pencils were handy, and the cousins set to work to write out half a dozen messages.

"We can set them floating on the river if nothing more," said Nellie. "Somebody might pick one up and act on it."

The hours slipped by, and from the quietness on board the girls guessed that some of their abductors had left the houseboat.

This was true. Baxter and Flapp had gone off, in company with Pick Loring, to send a message to Mrs. Stanhope and to Mrs. Laning, stating that Dora and Nellie were well and that they would be returned unharmed to their parents providing the sum of sixty thousand dollars be forwarded to a certain small place in the mountain inside of ten days.

"If you do not send the money the girls will suffer," the message concluded. "Beware of false dealings, or it may cost them their lives!"

"That ought to fetch the money," said Dan Baxter, after the business was concluded.

"If they can raise that amount," answered Loring. "Of course you know more about how they are fixed than I do."

"They can raise it—if they get the Rovers to aid them."

The prospects looked bright to the two horse thieves, and as soon as Loring returned to the houseboat he and Hamp Gouch applied themselves arduously to the liquor taken from Captain Starr's private locker.

"Those fellows mean to get drunk," whispered Lew Flapp, in alarm.

"I'm afraid so," answered Baxter. "But it can't be helped."

Late in the evening, much to their surprise, an old man in a dilapidated rowboat came up to the houseboat. It was Jake Shaggam, the hermit, who had been out fishing.

"How are ye, Shaggam!" shouted Pick Loring, who, on account of the liquor taken, felt extra sociable. "Come on board, old feller!"

Against the wishes of Baxter and Flapp, Jake Shaggam was allowed on board the houseboat and taken to the living room. Here he was given something to eat and drink and some tobacco.

77

"You're a good fellow, Jake," said Hamp Gouch. "Mighty good fellow. Show you something," and he took the old man to where the girls were locked in.

"Better stop this," said Flapp, in increased alarm.

"Oh, it's all right, you can trust Jake Shaggam," replied Gouch, with a swagger. Liquor had deprived him of all his natural shrewdness.

He insisted upon talking about the girls and tried to open the door. Failing in this he took the hermit around to the window.

"Nice old chap this is, gals," he said. "Finest old chap in old Kentucky. Think a sight o' him, I do. Shake hands with him."

"What are these yere gals doin' here?" asked Shaggam, with interest.

"Got 'em prisoners. Tell ye all 'bout it ter-morrow," answered Gouch, thickly. "Big deal on—better'n stealin' hosses."

"They seem to be very nice girls," answered Jake Shaggam. He was a harmless kind of an individual with a face that was far from repugnant.

Watching her chance Dora drew close to the old man.

"Take this, please do!" she whispered, and gave him one of the notes, folded in a dollar bill.

"Thank you," answered Jake Shaggam.

"Say nothing,—look at it as soon as you get away," added Dora.

The old hermit nodded, and in a few minutes more he followed Gouch to another part of the boat.

"Do you think he will deliver that message?" asked Nellie.

"Let us pray Heaven that he does," answered her cousin.

CHAPTER XXX

THE RESCUE—CONCLUSION

The Rovers and the others on the steam tug could scarcely wait for the old man in the dilapidated rowboat to come up alongside.

"You have a message for us?" said Dick. "Hand it over, quick."

"The message says as how you-uns will pay me twenty-five dollars fer delivering of it in twenty-four hours," said the old man, cautiously.

"Who is it from?"

"It is signed Dora Stanhope and Nellie Laning."

"Give it to me—I'll pay you the money," cried Tom.

"All right, reckon as how I kin trust you-uns," said the old man.

It was Jake Shaggam, who had received the message the evening before. He had read it with interest and started out at daylight to find out something about the Rovers and where they might be located. Good fortune had thrown him directly in our young friends' way.

"This is really a message from the girls!" cried Tom, reading it hastily. "It is in Nellie Laning's handwriting."

"And Dora Stanhope has signed her name too," added Dick. "I know her signature well."

"Of course you do," put in Fred, dryly, but nobody paid attention to the sally.

"They are on the houseboat, and the craft is hidden up Shaggam Creek," put in Sam. He turned to the captain of the tug. "Where is Shaggam Creek?"

"This ere is Shaggam Creek, an' I'm Jake Shaggam," answered the hermit. "But you-uns said you'd pay me thet twenty-five dollars."

"I will," said Tom, and brought out the amount at once.

"Thank you very much."

"If you'll take us to that houseboat without delay I'll give you another five dollars," put in Dick.

"I'll do it. But I don't want them fellers on the houseboat to see me."

"Why not?"

"Cos Pick Loring and Hamp Gouch thinks I am their friend. Ef they knowed as how I give 'em away they'd plug me full o' lead."

"Then the two horse thieves are with Baxter and Flapp," said Songbird. "If we bag the lot we'll be killing two birds with one stone, as the saying goes."

"Come on!" cried Paul Livingstone. "I want to get those two horse thieves by all means. Why, there is a reward of one thousand dollars for their capture, dead or alive."

"By golly, I'se out fo' dat reward!" came from Aleck, and he pulled out a horse pistol which he was carrying. "Jess let me see dem willains." And he flourished the weapon wildly.

The steam tug was led up the creek by Jake Shaggam for a distance of two miles.

"See that air turn yonder?" he said.

"Yes," said Captain Carson.

"Thet houseboat is behind the trees and bushes around the p'int. Now whar's the five dollars?"

"There you are," said Dick, and paid him.

"Much obliged. Now I reckon I'll go home an' let you-uns fight it out," added Jake Shaggam, and tying up his rowboat he stalked off, just as if he had accomplished nothing out of the ordinary.

"We had better approach with caution," said Paul Livingstone. "Those horse thieves are desperate characters. They would not be above shooting us down rather than give up to the law."

In the meantime Baxter and Flapp were much disturbed by the condition of affairs on board the houseboat. Both Loring and Gouch had been drinking more or less all night and were in far from a sober condition.

"I don't mind a drink myself, but those chaps make me sick," growled Dan Baxter.

"I guess we made a mistake to take them into our scheme," said Lew Flapp. "Look how Gouch blabbed to that old man last night."

"Where are they now?"

"In the captain's stateroom opening a new bottle of liquor. Neither of them can stand up straight."

"For two pins I'd pitch them overboard. Where is Sculley?"

"He is with them, drinking hard, too."

"If we only knew how to run that launch we could leave them behind and sail out of here."

"Perhaps we'll have to do that—if the three keep on drinking."

Baxter and Flapp were on deck. They had had their breakfast, but had given nothing more to the girls.

"I'm going to tame 'em," grumbled Flapp, who had not forgotten how the door had been slammed in his face.

"That's right, we'll make 'em come to terms," added Baxter. "We'll have 'em on their knees to us before we get through."

Presently both walked to the window of the stateroom Dora and Nellie occupied.

"Well, how do you feel—pretty hungry?" questioned Baxter.

"Not so very hungry?" said Dora, as lightly as she could.

"Don't you want a nice hot breakfast?"

"I'd rather have some fruit."

"Oh, by the way, we've got some nice harvest apples on board—and some berries. Wouldn't you like some berries, with sugar and cream?"

"And some fresh breakfast rolls?" put in Flapp.

"Not if you baked them," came from Nellie. "You can have a good breakfast, if you'll be a little more civil to us," resumed Dan Baxter.

"We are more civil than you deserve," said Dora.

"Do you want to be starved?"

At this both girls turned a trifle pale.

"Would you dare to starve us?" cried Nellie.

"Why not—if you won't be friendly?" asked Lew Flapp. "You've been treating us as if we were dogs."

"Yes, and we—" began Dan Baxter, when he chanced to look through the bushes and down the creek. "Great Scott, Flapp!" he yelled.

"What's up?"

"The game is up! Here comes a tug with the Rovers and a lot of other people on board!"

"The Rovers!" faltered Lew Flapp, and for the instant he shivered from head to feet.

"Oh, good! good!" cried Nellie. "Help!" she screamed. "Help!"

"Help! help!" added Dora. "Help us! This way!"

"We are coming!" came back, in Dick's voice, and a moment later the steam tug crashed into the side of the houseboat, and the Rovers and several others leaped on board.

"Stand where you are, Lew Flapp!" cried Tom, and rushed for the bully of Putnam Hall. "Stand, I say!" and then he hit Flapp a stunning blow in the ear which bowled the rascal over and over.

In the meantime Dan Baxter took to his heels and made for the front of the houseboat. From this point he jumped into the branches of a tree and disappeared from view.

"Come on after him!" cried Sam, and away he and Fred went after Baxter, leaving the others to take charge of Flapp, and round up the horse thieves and Sculley.

But Dan Baxter knew what capture meant—a long term of imprisonment in the future and, possibly, a good drubbing from the Rovers on the spot—and he therefore redoubled his efforts to escape.

"Follow me at your peril!" he sang out, and then they heard him crashing through the bushes. Gradually the sounds grew fainter and fainter.

"Where did he go to, Sam?"

"I can't say," said Sam. "We'll have to organize a regular party to run him down."

It was an easy matter to make Lew Flapp a prisoner. Once captured the former bully of the Hall blubbered like a baby.

"It was Dan Baxter led me into it," he groaned. "It was all his doings, not mine."

When Loring, Gouch, and Sculley were confronted by the party the intoxicated evil-doers were in no condition to offer any resistance. Roundly did they bewail their luck, but this availed them nothing, and without ceremony they were made prisoners, their hands being tied behind them with stout ropes.

"Are you hurt?" asked Dick, of the girls, anxiously.

"Not in the least, Dick," answered Dora. "But, oh! how thankful I am that you came as you did!"

"And I am thankful too," came from Nellie.

"And we are thankful to be on hand," said Tom.

And the others said the same.

Here let me bring to a close the story of "The Rover Boys on the River." The trip had been full of adventures, but it now looked as if all would end happily.

Without loss of time Dora and Nellie were taken care of and the houseboat was put into proper order for use by the Rovers and their friends.

"Dat galley am a mess to see," said Aleck Pop. "But I don't care—so long as dem young ladies am saved."

As speedily as possible, messages were sent to the Lanings and to Mrs. Stanhope, carrying the news of the girls' safety and the recovery of the missing houseboat. After that Paul Livingstone saw to it that Pick Loring, Hamp Gouch, and their accomplice, Sculley, were turned over to the proper authorities. For this the whole party received the reward of one thousand dollars, which was evenly divided between them.

"Dot's der first money I receive playing detecter," said Hans, when he got his portion. "Maybe I vos been a regular bolice detecter ven I got old enough, hey?"

Lew Flapp was taken back to New York State, to stand trial for the robbery of Aaron Fairchild's shop, but through the influence of his family and some rich friends he was let out on bail. When the time for his trial arrived he was missing.

"He is going to be as bad as Dan Baxter some day," said Sam.

"Perhaps; but he is more of a coward than Baxter," answered Dick.

"Wonder where Baxter disappeared to?" came from Tom.

"We'll find out some time," said Sam; and he was right. They soon met their old enemy again, and what Baxter did to bring them trouble will be told in the next volume of this series, to be entitled "The Rover Boys on the Plains; or, The Mystery of Red Rock Ranch." In this work we shall meet many of our old friends again and learn what they did towards solving a most unusual secret.

Two days after the missing houseboat was found there was a re-union on board in which all of our friends took part. There was a grand dinner, served in Aleck Pop's best style, and in the evening the craft was trimmed up with Japanese lanterns from end to end, and a professional orchestra of three pieces was engaged by the Rovers to furnish music for the occasion. Mr. Livingstone and his family visited the houseboat, bringing several young folks with them. The girls and boys sang, danced, and played games, while the older folks looked on. Songbird Powell recited several original poems, Fred Garrison made a really comic speech, and Hans Mueller convulsed everybody by his good nature and his funny way of talking.

"I never felt so light-hearted in my life!" said Tom, after the celebration had come to an end.

"We owe you and the others a great deal," said Mrs. Laning.

"Yes, and I shall not forget it," put in Mrs. Stanhope. "All of you are regular heroes!"

"Heroes? Pooh!" sniffed Tom. "Nothing of the sort. We are just wide-awake American boys."

And they are wide-awake; aren't they, kind reader?

THE END

CPSIA information can be obtained
at www.ICGtesting.com
Printed in the USA
BVHW062217010520
579061BV00013B/2523